A PULP FICTION TEXTBOOK

V.M. Devadas is a Malayalam writer, born in March 1981 in Wadakkancherry, Kerala. He has established himself as a leading voice in contemporary Malayalam fiction, having authored four novels and six collections of short stories. His writing is characterized by a unique stylistic flair, and he often delves into the political and philosophical dimensions of modern life. Devadas's works are known for their unconventional themes, which focus on the hybrid politics of people in our society. He is constantly experimenting with the structure, theme and narration of his works, which has earned him many accolades. He is the recipient of several prestigious awards, including the Kerala Sahitya Akademi Award, Malayala Manorama Novel Carnival Award, Swami Vivekananda Yuva Prathibha Award, O.V. Vijayan Memorial Literary Award and Vaikom Muhammad Basheer Malayala Padana Kendram Award, among others. Currently he is living in Chennai and working as an IT professional.

A PULP FICTION TEXTBOOK

(A Novel)

V.M. DEVADAS

hachette
INDIA

Originally published in Malayalam in 2009 as
Aaru Maranangalude Pulp Fiction Patapusthakam
First published in English in 2025 by Hachette India
(Registered name: Hachette Book Publishing India Pvt. Ltd)
An Hachette UK company
www.hachetteindia.com

1

Print ISBN 978-93-5731-400-8
Ebook ISBN 978-93-5731-836-5

Hachette Book Publishing India Pvt. Ltd
4th & 5th Floors, Corporate Centre,
Plot No. 94, Sector 44, Gurugram 122003, India

Typeset in Arno Pro 12/16
by R. Ajith Kumar, New Delhi

Printed and bound in India by Manipal Technologies Limited

FSC
www.fsc.org
MIX
Paper | Supporting responsible forestry
FSC™ C043100

To my family and friends,
who have been with me in both the tortoise's race
and the hare's slumber throughout my life.

The boundaries which divide Life from Death are at best shadowy and vague.
Who shall say where the one ends, and where the other begins?

– Edgar Allan Poe

Getting Started

Children who often listened to their grandmother's stories were familiar with the phrase, '...and they lived happily ever after'. They knew this ending was unrealistic and abrupt, which left them frustrated. Inevitably, they would ask, '...and then?'

To address this never-ending question of '...and then', new stories emerged. In these tales, characters died or vanished mysteriously. Textbooks may have been designed similarly. They focused on deaths and disappearances to avoid the question.

However, this approach didn't solve the problem. In classrooms today, students still pose the same challenging question. Despite deliberate attempts to silence this curiosity through narratives of definitive endings and abrupt vanishings, the old question persists: '...and then?'

Forewarning

A. None of the characters in this book are named.
B. The textbook on deaths lacks descriptions of nature.
C. The definitions and details in this book should not be considered authoritative.

Disclaimer:

This book, despite featuring many emotional and suspenseful moments, scatters them across chapters or presents them in the epistolary structure of a textbook.

Instead of a detailed narrative explaining the storyline, the content is a concise, textbook-style description.

As a result, it falls upon the reader to piece together these moments and comprehend them within their relevant contexts.

You can proceed to the next chapter without completing the exercises. However, it is advisable to complete the exercises before moving on.

Contents

Life is a puzzle made of moments and time.

Let's arrange the pieces to reveal the rhyme.

A
PULP FICTION
TEXT BOOK

1

Let's Learn New Things!

The following news reports from 2009 serve as the entry point for this textbook.

Maoist Leader Killed in Encounter with Police

Kochi: A Maoist was killed during an encounter with the police. Acting on a tip-off received by the SI of North Station, police cordoned off a hideout on the city outskirts. The Maoist opened fire on the policemen while attempting to escape but was killed in the ensuing encounter. Police discovered Maoist pamphlets and weapons upon searching the area. Preliminary information suggests the deceased is a wanted Maoist leader.

Husband and Wife Die in Tragic Accidents

Kochi: A customs officer died in a road accident on his way home after receiving news of his wife's accidental death. His wife had fallen from the third floor of their house and was rushed to the hospital but did not survive. The officer was fatally injured while returning home to mourn his wife's loss. Police suspect a hit-and-run and have not yet identified the vehicle involved.

Electronics Shop Owner Shoots Himself in Godown

New Delhi: A shocking suicide case came to light in Palika Bazar. An electronics shop owner allegedly shot himself in the head in his firm's godown. Employees discovered his body on Tuesday morning when they arrived for work. Police said the shop owner had closed his shop on Monday night and sent his staff home. He then went to the godown on the first floor of the same building and shot himself with an unlicensed pistol. Police also recovered a licensed revolver from his possession. The reason for the suicide remains unknown. The shop owner did not leave a suicide note or any clue indicating why he took this extreme step. He was reportedly doing well in his business and had no apparent financial or personal troubles. A suicide case has been registered, and further investigation is underway.

Girl Sentenced for Selling Sex Toys at School Dies after Jumping from Police Van

New Delhi: A 17-year-old girl, arrested for allegedly selling artificial sex devices at her school and engaging in unnatural sex, died after jumping out of a police van on Wednesday. Police stated that the girl, sentenced to two years, escaped custody while being transported to a juvenile home. She suffered severe head and spinal injuries and was taken to a nearby hospital but succumbed to her wounds. The doctor who performed the surgery noted that a delay in obtaining blood from the rare HH group also contributed to her death. The girl, an orphan from Santhome Orphanage, had been accused of supplying sex toys to her schoolmates and engaging in unnatural sexual practices.

Palika Bazar to Undergo Renovation Ahead of Commonwealth Games

Delhi: As Delhi prepares for the upcoming Commonwealth Games, Palika Bazar, infamous as a grey market, is set for a major makeover. The infamous underground market is notorious for selling counterfeit products, pirated DVDs, illegal sex toys and hidden cameras, among other dubious items. It has also been a source of law-and-order problems in the city, with incidents of eve-teasing, harassment and illegal trade. Officials have announced that funds have been allocated in the budget for Palika Bazar's renovation. This will include improvements in ventilation, lighting, security and cleanliness. The officials hope these changes will help transform the market's image and attract more customers.

Exercise

I. Please write a brief news report using the information, given in bits and pieces, below.

(The answers may vary based on personal and political perspectives. Some may prioritize the severity of the natural disaster, while others may focus more on government involvement and support.)

Earthquake – Magnitude 6.8 – Coastal region – Damage: Buildings, Roads, Power, Communication – Government's involvement – Rescue efforts

Ans:

Title: Coastal Region Devastated By A Strong Earthquake

Report: A powerful earthquake measuring 6.8 on the Richter scale has devastated the coastal region. The tremor caused buildings to collapse and triggered panic among the residents. The roads are blocked by debris, making it difficult to reach the affected areas, and the power and communication networks have also been severely damaged. The government has already started the evacuation process and promised to provide more support to the affected region, offering important resources to help with the recovery. Rescue teams are working tirelessly to find and assist the people affected by this natural disaster.

II. Do you think everything in news reports is true? Let's assume you're a field reporter. What methods will you choose for basic fact-checking?

Ans:

1. *Get information directly from people who saw or experienced the event, as well as from experts, to make sure you have accurate information.*
2. *Look at official documents and records, like reports from the government or court documents, to check if the facts are true.*
3. *Check information from different reliable sources to make sure the details match up and to avoid any biases.*
4. *Use trusted fact-checking organizations and websites.*
5. *Ask experts who have knowledge about a specific topic for their opinions and knowledge, especially if the subject is complicated or technical.*

III. What does the term post-truth mean? Could you provide some examples?

Ans:

Post-truth means that people care more about what they feel and believe than what is true. Sometimes, news can be changed or twisted to match what someone wants to say or do. Post-truth can make people ignore the truth and trust wrong information or 'fake news', where people's feelings and opinions can be more powerful than facts. Examples of post-truth include political manipulations, media bias, propaganda, the anti-vaccine movement, stereotyping a particular community, fake encounters, the blame game during a crisis and the use of red herring reports to divert attention from actual issues.

Before the Dantewada massacre and Burkapal[1] *attack took place...*

And before the formation of Green Hunt and Greyhounds[2]*...*

[1] Naxalite ambushes

[2] Anti-Naxal special armed forces

2

A Maoist Eulogy

Contrary to the news, I wonder how I can disclose the truth of my staged death...

Two years ago, I left my home country to work in Hong Kong. I gradually lost touch with most of my old friends. However, one friend managed to find my address and started sending me letters. This friend was my college buddy, a person with big ambitions and an impressive way with words. Yet, as I read his letters, I noticed a significant difference. They lacked the vitality that had once defined his communication. It was as if he had become a completely different person. I wondered what had caused this change in him.

After a few exchanges, he asked a strange question: 'Are you married yet?'

In jest, I replied, 'No, I'm just living with a few synthetic companions and occasionally enjoying the company of Mongolian beauties.' It was meant to be light-hearted, but to my surprise, he took my words seriously.

His next letter had an even stranger request: 'Could you send me a sex doll? I really need one.'

I was shocked and couldn't understand why he would ask for such a thing. What had happened to him? Was he lonely, depressed or desperate? I struggled with how to answer his request. Little did I know that this would be the start of a strange and twisted story that would change our lives forever.

I wasn't aware that sex toys were banned in India. One day, while shopping at a mall, I purchased a sex doll designed for vaginal and oral sex. Made of synthetic material, it had the skin colour of a Mongolian woman. Its crystal eyes remained open all the time, which was a bit unsettling. When I inspected it before buying it, there were no defects. However, when I inflated it using the air pump connected to its vagina, the wrinkled skin became smooth like that of a young woman. The artificial vagina, anus, mouth and other sexual organs were all precisely and realistically designed. The salesman, who spoke fluent English, explained how to take care of it and how to clean it after use.

The sex doll I had sent my friend as a prank was seized by customs at the International Air Parcels. That's how I learned that sex toys were illegal in India. Interestingly, he never mentioned the incident in his subsequent letters. Instead, he poured out his thoughts and emotions, sharing the lingering pain of a past love affair that continued to haunt him. He wrote about his struggles with reclaiming his passion for literature, as well as his fascination with the Maoist movements in India and neighbouring countries. His letters covered a range of topics, but they all revealed his deep desperation. He seemed to find comfort and escape from his misery in radical left-wing ideologies. Although I didn't necessarily agree with his views, I avoided judging him and tried to understand his perspective.

Later, after mentioning the doll, he wrote that it was good that it was seized by the Customs Department during checking. He believed benefit accrued when it was withheld rather than when it was received. I couldn't comprehend the reasoning behind his statement. I was even more confused when, a month later, he changed his mind and asked me to send another sex doll, identical to the first one, to an orphanage address in Delhi. His letters often puzzled me, making it hard to fully understand his intentions.

I'm still trying to understand why I was killed – why my life was abruptly taken from me. I didn't have enough time to truly live, explore and experience all that life offers. I hadn't grown tired of seeing the beauty of Mongolian women, with their slim figures, appealing almond-shaped eyes and light skin. I'm left with many questions.

- When did I think about going back to my home country?
- When did I consider visiting him at his remote, isolated home?
- And when did I decide to become his friend, if I ever did?

These unanswered questions trouble me, leaving me confused and yearning for understanding.

As I approached the small house, I noticed that my friend had changed a lot since college. Books and clothes were scattered everywhere, and the room was dusty with cobwebs. It was strikingly different from his college hostel room. The room's state seemed to mirror his current life and appearance. When I asked why he lived far from the newspaper office, he said it was to avoid crowds.

Despite his reclusive nature, he kindly offered me tea, and we chatted pleasantly. But before I had finished drinking it, he suddenly began to change his clothes, grabbed a bag and rushed out, claiming he had to visit a friend urgently. I offered him a ride in my rented car, but he refused, insisting on keeping the visit secret. He asked me if I could give him the car keys, saying he would easily make his way back. I couldn't understand why he avoided me. (*Or perhaps I don't understand anything at all.*)

He took the keys and left, leaving me alone. The house had no TV or radio for entertainment. Only scattered books, messy notes and used clothes lay around. Uncomfortable in my tight pants, I wore his *mundu*[3] and tried reading a book while sitting on the floor. The book was about Naxalite ideology, but it didn't hold my interest. I closed it and looked outside instead. I saw cattle grazing in a nearby swamp, with crows riding on their backs. The legs of the quadrupeds were half-buried in mud. Above the clattering hooves of the cattle, I heard the roar of a speeding vehicle.

I was surprised by the quick return, but it wasn't my car – it was a police jeep. A few constables got

[3] A traditional garment worn around the waist in South India

out and started searching. Only the sub-inspector stayed in the vehicle. When I asked him what was happening, he shocked me by slapping my face and asking a strange question, 'Where have you hidden the sex doll in this house?'

I didn't understand the question or what was going on. Yes, I had sent him sex dolls a couple of times. One got held up at a foreign post office, and I don't know what happened to the second one. The question was not about why I sent the sex doll but where I kept it in that house, which didn't even belong to me.

'Sir, I think this matter is bigger than what we thought earlier. It doesn't seem like we can leave this place any time soon.'

A constable approached the sub-inspector, holding a cardboard box filled with books and scribbles. I was even more astonished when the constable took out a locally made gun from the box. The inspector's face brightened as if he had won the lottery. When I tried to explain that I wasn't the one they were investigating and that this wasn't my house, they slapped me harder than before.

I couldn't fully comprehend the situation. In my confusion, I wondered how to explain my circumstances to the police. Suddenly, my legs betrayed me and I started running. My heart raced with anxiety as I struggled to find a way out. The sub-inspector pulled his gun from the holster on his waist and fired at my back. I stumbled and fell into one of the muddy footprints left by cattle climbing hastily from the muddy ground. The inspector might have aimed for my knee or leg, but his shot must have gone off when I slipped and began to fall. My lifeless body lay there for a couple of hours. After a thorough search inside the house, a constable approached and placed a gun in my hand. By then, he likely noticed that rigor mortis had set in, and my fingers were slightly stiff.

Oh, how quickly events can change course. I had merely been visiting an old friend, and now I had become a deceased victim of a fake encounter. The police officers stood there with triumph evident on their faces.

I am lying there, lifeless, after being shot.
Who let the cattle climb up the muddy ground?
What the hell is happening around me?
Where did he go with my car?
Why did he keep a gun in his house?
I don't understand any of this...

Exercise

I. Let's assume that you have been appointed as a lawyer to prove the fake encounter incident in this chapter in court. What would be the five key points to win the case in your favour?

Ans:

1. ***Location of the gunshot wound:*** *The location of the gunshot wound on the victim's body could indicate whether the victim was facing the police or not. If the wound is on the back, it would suggest that the victim did not pose an immediate threat.*
2. ***Autopsy report:*** *The autopsy report could provide crucial evidence about the trajectory of the bullet, the distance from which the shot was fired and other details that could support or contradict the police's version of events.*
3. ***Police procedure:*** *An examination of whether the police followed proper procedure during the encounter, such as issuing a warning before opening fire, could indicate whether the encounter was justified or not.*
4. ***Forensic evidence:*** *Forensic evidence, such as gunshot residue analysis, could help determine whether the victim was shot at close range or from a distance. This analysis can also provide crucial data about whether the victim fired any bullets before being attacked.*

It could corroborate or contradict the police's version of events.

5. ***Witness testimony:*** *Witness testimony could provide valuable evidence about what actually happened during the encounter. Even if there are no eyewitnesses present at the location during the incident, it would be helpful if someone residing nearby, or any passer-by, could confirm the number of gunshots heard and the interval between each one.*

II. This chapter refers to cattle grazing on the marshland. Can you write a poem in this context?

Ans:

Green blades sway, they wander and roam,
A world of their own, a place to call home.
The fields stretch wide, an expanse to explore,
Free to graze and wander, their voices implore.
Nature's embrace, a balm to their soul,
A peaceful refuge, where they're free to extol.
As they graze and roam, a message is clear,
For our future held dear, a world to revere.

III. List some controversial police encounters in India and briefly analyse their social impact.

1. The **Ishrat Jahan** case involved the killing of four people by the Gujarat police in 2004. The police claimed it was an encounter with terrorists. Later investigations questioned the authenticity of the encounter, suggesting it might have been staged. The case became highly politicized, with debates about Ishrat's innocence or involvement in terrorist activities.
2. In 2005, **Sohrabuddin Sheikh** was killed in an alleged fake encounter by the Gujarat and Rajasthan police. His wife, **Kausar Bi**, disappeared and was later found dead. The case gained national attention due to allegations of political involvement. It led to several high-profile arrests.
3. **Tulsiram Prajapati**, an associate of Sohrabuddin Sheikh, was killed in another alleged fake encounter in 2006. His death was linked to the Sohrabuddin case. There were claims that he was eliminated because he was a key witness. The case highlighted concerns about police misconduct and extrajudicial killings.
4. The **Manipur Extrajudicial Killings** refer to numerous alleged fake encounters in Manipur over several decades. Human rights organizations have reported hundreds of such cases. These often involved security forces operating

under the Armed Forces (Special Powers) Act, 1958. The incidents led to widespread protests and demands for justice in the state.

5. The **Hyderabad Encounter** of 2019 involved the killing of four men accused of rape and murder by the Telangana police. The police claimed the suspects were shot while trying to escape during a crime scene reconstruction. Some praised the police action as swift justice. Others raised concerns about due process and the rule of law.

These cases have sparked debates about police accountability, human rights and the balance between security and civil liberties in India. They have led to various investigations, court cases and public discussions about police reforms. The controversies have highlighted the complex relationship between law enforcement, politics and justice in the country.

IV. Write a short essay on the Naxalite/Maoist movements in India, including an analysis of the government's efforts to counter these insurgencies.

Ans:

The Maoist movement is a political ideology that originated in China and is based on the ideas of communist leader Mao

Zedong. It gained popularity in China during the Chinese Civil War and eventually led to the establishment of the People's Republic of China in 1949. The movement spread to other countries, including India, where it gave rise to the Naxalite movement. The Naxalite movement is a left-wing extremist movement that emerged in the late 1960s in the village of Naxalbari in West Bengal with the aim of overthrowing the Indian government and establishing a communist state. The movement has been involved in several violent incidents and has been designated as a terrorist organization by the Indian government. Some of the major events associated with the Naxalite movement include the Naxalbari uprising, the Srikakulam armed struggle and the Maoist insurgency in central India. The Communist Party of India (Maoist) is one of the major parties associated with the Naxalite movement.

The government has taken several measures to counter the Naxalite/Maoist movement. Some of the major tasks undertaken by the government and security forces include:

1. **Deployment of security forces:** The government has deployed a large number of security forces in Naxalite-affected areas to combat the insurgency.
2. **Development initiatives:** The government has launched several development initiatives in Naxalite-affected areas

to address the root causes of the insurgency, such as poverty, lack of education and lack of access to basic services.

3. **Surrender and rehabilitation policy:** The government has implemented a surrender and rehabilitation policy to encourage Naxalites to lay down their arms and join the mainstream.
4. **Coordination between states:** The government has encouraged coordination between states affected by the Naxalite movement to share intelligence and resources to combat insurgency.
5. **Use of technology:** The government uses technology to gather intelligence and monitor Naxalite activities.

V. What are the major technologies used by the government to counter the Naxalite/Maoist movement? Please mention the key items and explain their significance in addressing this issue.

Ans:

1. Motion and thermal sensor cameras: They monitor movements and detect unusual activities, especially in forest areas.
2. Drones and aerial surveillance: These provide real-time data and imagery of remote areas.

3. *Phone tapping and communication interception: These are used to monitor communications of suspected individuals.*
4. *Geographic Information System (GIS): They analyse spatial data related to suspicious activities and areas of influence.*
5. *Data analytics: This involves processing huge amounts of data collected from surveillance methods.*

Prior to the changes that reshaped Palika Bazar before the Commonwealth Games...

In a time preceding the rise of the Aam Aadmi Party to political power in Delhi...

3

The Merchant of Palika Bazar

Contrary to the news report, I am discussing my murder because you found me with a gun in my mouth and assumed that I had shot myself.

You must believe me. The bullet from the gun in my hand did not smash my head open. I did not take my own life. Think about it: Wouldn't it make more sense for me to have been shot with my own foreign-made gun, usually kept in the table drawer at the cash counter, rather than this locally made one? There is no other logical explanation. I urge you to trust me. Despite my overweight body and the sinister look from the wrinkles on my forehead, the result of years of intense calculations, I have always been honest in my business dealings, before and after my death.

Imagine entering Palika Bazar as though you're entering a secret chamber, rich with filthy treasures and hidden passageways. There are six open entrances to the bazar, while the seventh remains closed. This set-up resembles the seven energy points, or chakras, in our bodies. Tragically, a bullet once pierced my Sahasrara Padma – the Crown Lotus – resulting in my death as it tore through my bald head. As a result, the previously sealed seventh door has now opened, creating a new way into Palika Bazar.

I have often perceived the current state of Palika Bazar to resemble that of a weary, middle-aged prostitute, languid with laziness. It was once a bustling urban courtesan, catering to the entire city's population, warmly welcoming all who entered. It was during this time that my father decided to open an electronics shop in Palika Bazar, following the closure of his fabric shops in Karol Bagh and Khanna Market. He abruptly declared, 'Hey, listen, this is the age of electronics.' I had come there to assist my father when my studies were put on hold due to my violent and boozy college days. Since then, three-quarters of my life has been spent in this underground air-conditioned market.

After its initial charm faded, Palika Bazar slowly turned into a grey market for smuggled goods. Our shop, Electro Hut, became infamous for selling pirated or smuggled items. We offered cheap high-end electronics, foreign movie cassettes, video games and various other products. Palika Bazar was a refuge for those escaping Delhi's scorching summer heat. It provided a wide array of goods, attracting both locals and foreign tourists. This mix of visitors added to the market's vibrant atmosphere. Our new business was thriving, but then tragedy struck. My father passed away suddenly, leaving me as the sole owner of the shop. Around the same time, I also got married.

I never compromised on food or sex. Both spicy and sweet foods, as well as alluring women, were irresistible to me. There was a time when I spent more time with other women than with my wife. Am I calculating this correctly, or am I missing something? Despite being a businessman, math challenges me. Without calculators or accountants, my business wouldn't survive. I've noticed a recurring problem – when I write numbers with more than three digits, at least one digit often changes from one line to the next. This leads to incorrect calculations and inaccurate figures.

These days, many seedy faces and vulgar expressions greet visitors to this underground bazar. This implies that the vendors look unsavoury and may engage in illegal or immoral activities. It's amazing how quickly things change. Palika has transformed from a queen's chamber into a murky harem. In just fifteen years, Delhi's once-best bazar has become a filthy grey market. Today, visitors to this underground bazar encounter many shady characters.

In the XXX series, you'll see various products and their display posters. Vendors might approach you saying, 'What do you want, sir? We have everything – solo, couple, threesome, lesbian, gay, bestial... Sir, would you like a dildo or vibrator for your girlfriend? We also have latex dolls. You won't find them elsewhere. They might even be better than your girlfriend or wife. Interested in buying anything, sir?'

If these questions shock you, it's probably your first visit to Palika Bazar. Look at the vendors' expressions as they approach you. You'll notice their façade. They might make you question your own stamina and performance in bed, possibly make you feel inadequate. Then, they might lead you to a high-end or electronics store. There, you'll find various items, including CDs, dildos and even sex dolls. Doesn't it feel like you've entered Alice's Wonderland, far from Delhi's usual hustle? (*If you're unsure whether you're in a fetish-fantasy land or Palika Bazar, you can pinch yourself to check. But please don't pinch the latex skin of the sex dolls or the soft dildo.*)

I, too, find myself trapped within the glass walls of a wonderland. Have you ever thought about a crystal barrier that's both a wall and a lens? On one side, you see many tempting things, but you can't reach them. How would you feel in such a situation?

Example 1: Imagine you're hungry and can't find food. Now, picture yourself trapped inside unbreakable glass walls. On the other side are huge portions of spicy, delicious dishes. How would you feel?
(*No need to answer quickly. This example isn't very relevant. Don't waste any time thinking about it.*)

Example 2: What if you have indigestion and can't eat even a small amount? How would you react to seeing the glass walls and the tempting food on the other side?
(*Let's think about this scenario for a moment before moving on.*)

As Palika Bazar became a grey market for illicit goods, several personal changes took place:

A. *My health declined, leading to diabetes due to an unhealthy body mass index.*
B. *I developed erectile dysfunction because of severe diabetes.*
C. *My sexual satisfaction turned to despair, like a ship stranded on a deserted island.*
D. *My electronics shop has changed a lot. It became a glass case that sells artificial sexual devices and sex dolls.*

None of these circumstances were a matter of choice. My lifestyle and circumstances imposed A, B and C upon me, while my wife originated the idea of D. The combination of reasons B and C led to my failure in the bedroom. Regarding C, my wife felt like an unattainable island, while I was a shipwrecked sailor adrift in the vast sea. The relentless waves and swells pushed us further apart with each passing day. To bridge the gap, I once purchased a toy from a nearby shop in the bazar as a gift for my wife. Although the island was expecting the arrival of a ship with powerful logos on its flags, a long-barrelled telescope made of brass, a lot of merchandise and noisy sailors, one could assume that even a tired sailor washed ashore on a broken plank would receive a warmer welcome from that remote island.

My wife was aware of the transformation and events taking place at Palika Bazar. She was the first to question why vibrators shouldn't be sold to make the shop profitable, just like others were doing. While I may not excel in maths and profit calculations, the blood of generations of business traditions runs through our family. Consequently, artificial sexual devices were also sold in my shop, which led to Palika Bazar becoming more obscene.

How do I get artificial sexual devices?

These toys are usually smuggled from China, Singapore and Malaysia. Most shops at Palika use this route. But some people, including me, get them differently. It's cheaper and less risky. Do you think all the vibrators, sex dolls, vacuum pumps, phallus rings and porn caught in customs are destroyed? No. Less than 20 per cent are destroyed for show. Crawford Market in Mumbai and Palika Bazar in Delhi are the main destinations for these items. There are shady, illegal ways to get them from customs and foreign post offices. I organize their distribution through these channels. Some agents arrange this for a cheaper margin.

How did I get to meet that particular girl?

One day, three girls visited my shop. They looked about fifteen to seventeen years old, not regular Palika Bazar customers. When I saw them touching various electronic gadgets, I quickly understood why they were there. A good seller can read customers' expressions and guess their needs in Palika Bazar. I brought out the items they wanted from the shop's storage area. I displayed a range of sex toys on the glass table. As I explained how to use each toy, all three blushed with embarrassment. They were all adorable, but I paid extra attention to one girl. She looked scared and was sweating despite the air conditioning.

Why did I pay special attention to only one of the three girls?

A. Petite body.
B. Frightened facial expression.
C. Long, trembling fingers resembling a vibrator.
D. None of these.

Is she Ambalika[4] in Palika?

She stood alone in a corner, still and reserved, unlike her two friends who were busy exploring the sex toys. She seemed almost frozen, like a high-end latex doll, watching her friends press buttons and rummage through devices. Only one girl bought something, a Fetish Dye. They left, but moments later, she returned, seemingly braver, and asked, 'How much is that pink butterfly?'

'It's called the Fluttering Butterfly. It's a vibrator. It costs three thousand rupees, but I can discount it to two thousand. Shall I pack it?'

'I don't have money now. I was just asking.'

'I think you want to buy, but cheaper. How about a different, less expensive dildo?'

'No, I want the pink butterfly. But I have no money.'

'Well, there's only one left. You could break in at night and steal your favourite pink butterfly or filch some money from your parents.'

'To steal from my parents, I'd have to steal my parents first.'

---

[4] An Indian epic character who was abducted by Bhishma for his brother and became the royal mother of a blind king of the Kuru Dynasty

'?'

'I'm not like the others. I'm from Santhome Orphanage. I'm telling you because I love the pink butterfly so much.'

I looked at her again, noting the colour of her uniform and the details on her ID card. At that moment, I thought she might be lying for these reasons:

(a) *She might be eliciting sympathy to get the pink toy for free.*

(b) *The name of the school on her ID card was quite prestigious. How could an orphan attend such a posh school?*

I didn't want to lose money, but how could I refuse a girl her age? So, I decided to be more generous.

'Listen, girl... I can't afford to lose money. I can only offer a discount. But there's another way. Interested in a deal?'

'?'

'I have some devices for you. I'll give them one by one, except the pink butterfly. Can you sell them at school? You'll get 5 per cent commission on each sale. When your commission equals the butterfly's price, it's yours. This deal has two benefits for you.

(*a*) *You can use the devices before selling if you keep them clean and undamaged. Don't tell customers this.*

(b) *You can get the Fluttering Butterfly without paying for it.*

But remember... Don't try to cheat me. If you do, I'll be at your school gate or orphanage door. I'm offering you a fair deal. Deal?'

'Deal.' She nodded in agreement before leaving the store for the second time, carrying a packet of 'Ben Wa Balls' in her bag.

We had a fair-trade deal. Within a month, she earned enough commission to get the Fluttering Butterfly as agreed. But she didn't show up on the promised day to collect it. She also didn't pay me for the last item she took for secret sales. Since the toy's price was much lower than her commission amount, I didn't mind the broken deal. A few days later, I read a newspaper report about the sales of sex toys in a school. It involved a student acting as an agent. I felt very guilty when I learnt she had been arrested. However, I didn't try to rescue her because any such action would have implicated me in the case.

Now, let's discuss my murder. A man arrived just as the shop was about to close for the night. When I told him we were closed, he showed me his identity card. He was a customs officer. I admit I was scared by the sudden raid. He grabbed his gun, pointed it at my head and took me to the godown. I don't know why, but he warned me before putting the gun in my mouth. He said, 'Never again sell pink butterflies to girls. Okay?' Then he shot me.

(*Please tell my family to cover my coffin well. When I'm fully covered, I feel safe. It reminds me of the comfort I felt wrapping myself in a blanket during the days I was depressed. The blanket also helps me avoid the sights on the other side of the crystal wall.*)

Exercise

I. In this chapter, you learned that the Merchant of Palika presented various sex toys in front of the girls who visited his shop. Let's jot down the names, and the advantages and disadvantages of some of the toys he might have exhibited to them.

Fluttering Butterfly: *This small, discreet toy is easy to use and popular. It provides pinpoint clitoral stimulation. It's fragile and has low battery life.*

Wand Vibrator: *This powerful, versatile toy works for both external and internal stimulation. Some users might find it large and bulky. Its intensity may be too much for others.*

Dildo: *This toy offers realistic stimulation for various orifices. Users need to choose the right size and shape for optimal pleasure.*

Kegel Balls: *These help strengthen pelvic muscles and improve sexual health and pleasure. They don't provide direct stimulation and can be tricky to insert and remove.*

Rabbit Vibrator: *This is a comparatively costly toy that stimulates both the clitoris and G-spot. It works for internal and external use.*

Suction Toy: This provides intense, unique clitoral stimulation and can lead to multiple orgasms. The toy is often expensive.

Fetish Die: This toy has a long wire with a vibrator at one end and a six-sided die at the other. The vibration mode changes based on which button is pressed on each side of the die.

Strapless Strap-on: This toy can pleasure both partners and allows for various adventurous activities. Some may find it challenging to use. It may not fit all body types.

Nipple Clamps: These enhance foreplay and work for BDSM play. They can provide pleasurable sensations. However, if not adjusted properly, they can be painful or uncomfortable. They may not suit all body types.

Ben Wa Balls: These strengthen pelvic muscles and enhance pleasure. They don't offer direct stimulation and can be difficult to insert and remove.

II. Write a short note on Palika Bazar, highlighting its history and recent transformation.

Palika Bazar, an underground market in Connaught Place, Delhi, emerged in the 1970s. It was designed as a commercial hub to decongest the main market. Initially, it offered a variety of affordable goods, attracting many customers. Over time, Palika Bazar gained a notorious reputation. Its maze-like structure facilitated illegal activities. It became known for counterfeit goods, pirated software and other contraband items. This association with shady deals and unethical practices tarnished the market's image. There were even a couple of murders that took place at Palika Bazar.

In recent years, efforts have been made to transform Palika Bazar. Authorities have cracked down on illegal activities. They've also improved infrastructure and introduced new shops and brands. Despite ongoing challenges, the market is gradually shedding its negative image. It now aims to become a legitimate shopping destination.

III. Draw a map of Palika Bazar.

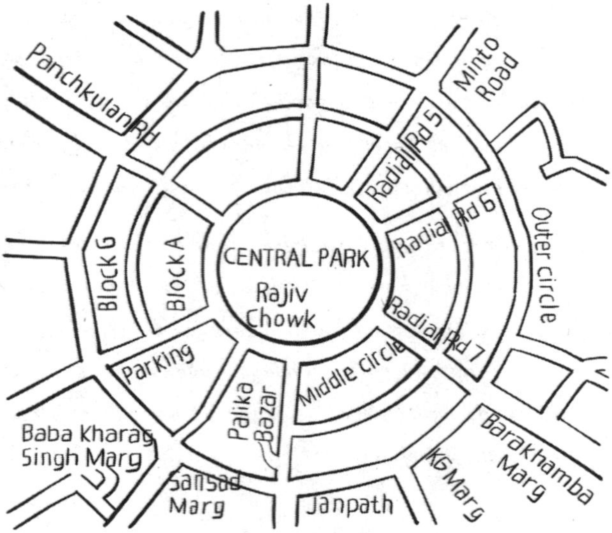

Before online shopping portals became popular in India and started selling sex toys labelled as personal massagers or wellness devices...

4

Alone in Wonderland

Despite what the news may say, the truth about my planned murder is that...

Before I start my story, I'd like to clarify a few points:

a. My tale will unfold in a cyclical or recursive manner.
b. It begins with a vehicle accident that results in my parents' deaths.
c. It ends with another accident, leading to my own death.
d. There's a nine-year gap between these two accidents.

Let me try to begin like this...
'I lost my parents in a car accident.'

Ah! That's not a good start. I've made a couple of mistakes:

1. I've already revealed how the story begins and ends.
2. I didn't start in the style of a sympathy-seeking teenager.

You might know me as the 'agent who sold sex toys in school' from news reports. To overcome any prejudices and evoke compassion, I need to use language effectively. I'll draw on my teenage innocence and emotional depth to challenge your preconceptions.

So, here's how I'll start the story...

'I lost my dearest papa and mama forever in a car accident that took place when I was a child.'

Only seven, I was the sole survivor of that accident. While recovering in the hospital and during my journey to Santhome Orphanage, I realized several things:

1. My businessman father was trapped in massive debt.
2. Some people suspected my father caused the accident intentionally.
3. Both families disapproved of my parents' interfaith marriage.

4. My father's arrogance and extravagance caused rifts with both families. As a result, my mother and I lived in isolation.
5. For these reasons, no one wanted to be my guardian.
6. From now on, I was an orphan.

The second part of my story begins as I arrive at Santhome Orphanage from the hospital. I want to clarify that while linguistic, rhetorical and age-related elements may be present, I don't intend to deceive. If I did, I would have changed the orphanage's name from 'Santhome' to 'Marian' for a more feminine tone. 'Santhome' comes from Saint Thomas, while 'Marian' relates to the Virgin Mary. The rhetorical and age-related elements that should help my storytelling are currently hindering me. I may change my narration tone at any time in the passages below.

Life continued at Santhome Orphanage with other orphans. Despite sharing a living space, fear and selfishness existed among the girls when sharing essentials like food and clothes.
(*Santhome Orphanage caters exclusively to girls, hence the repeated phrase 'one girl, another girl.'*)

I was lucky to have a sponsor who saved me from such fears. I called him 'Sponsor Uncle,' as Mother instructed. She emphasized that I should love and respect him because sponsorship was a privilege other Santhome girls didn't have. This support gave me better clothes, education and other advantages compared to my fellow orphans. I could continue attending the same expensive school.

You may have noticed that I referred to someone as 'Mother.' I used this term for the nun who ran Santhome. If I wanted to create a more favourable atmosphere, I could have depicted Mother as cruel. But that wouldn't be accurate. In reality, she was truly like a mother to me. She had a special affection for nine out of twenty-three Santhome orphans, including me. The reason was that these nine children were considered beautiful. Mother would often call us 'my dear angels...'

If I wanted to create a rhetorical effect again, I could have included myself in the group of fourteen instead of the nine angels. However, even if I were in the fourteen, you wouldn't notice any difference between the groups. Despite being called angels, we didn't receive preferential treatment in food or accommodation compared to the other fourteen. The fourteen had no reason to be jealous. Instead,

Mother would comb our hair, adorn it with colourful ribbons, call us angels, kiss our cheeks before bedtime and give us glow-in-the-dark rosaries. These were the only special considerations from Mother.

At Santhome, I received birthday gifts, cards, chocolates and clothes from Sponsor Uncle every year by courier. This sponsorship allowed me to continue at one of Delhi's top schools. Despite attending a different school, it didn't cause significant jealousy among other Santhome residents. Although there were noticeable differences – my ID card, uniform, earlier departure and later return, heavier workload – the others didn't pay much attention. Another difference was my textbooks. Consequently, while the twenty-two Santhome residents in the same class studied together and helped each other, I had to tackle my homework and assignments alone.

Apart from birthdays, Sponsor Uncle occasionally sent gifts. There's an important detail I haven't mentioned yet. I didn't want to seem boastful, so I kept it to myself for a while. The truth is, I have a talent for painting. I can create beautiful landscapes, portraits and various objects, but my speciality is drawing butterflies. When I colour them, I prefer using pink. Sponsor Uncle started sending me crayons, paints and brushes because Mother sent him some of my pictures. While other residents might have felt jealous when I received these gifts, my inclination to share helped me avoid hostility.

The next phase began when I experienced my first period at thirteen. After Sunday mass, I returned to Santhome and started a watercolour painting of two large pink butterflies. As I coloured the first butterfly, I realized the pink paint was running out, but I continued working. Suddenly, I felt a dull ache in my lower abdomen. I had gotten my period... The pain wasn't as severe as I had expected it to be. However, I often experienced abdominal pain when bending over while painting for a long time.

Oh! Where did I stop? Hmm... Yes, the paintings... As usual, the paintbrush glided across the paper, following my pencil markings. However, this time, something unexpected happened. A drop of paint spread beyond the intended boundaries. Anxious and urgent, I hastily entered Mother's room without knocking. To my surprise, she was talking to someone else. I gestured that I had something important to say. She excused herself and turned to me. But instead of addressing my concerns, she guided me outside and scolded me for two reasons:

1. Entering without permission when a guest was present.
2. Spilling colour on my cream-coloured dress while painting.

She advised me not to be arrogant and careless, thinking I had many clothes due to the sponsorship. I told her that I was attentive while drawing and mentioned it wasn't the pink palette that stained my dress. Suddenly, Mother smiled. Kissing my forehead, she said, 'My little angel has grown up. I will no longer call you an angel. Now you have become the Virgin Mary.'

I assume you understand about periods now. It involves the transition of Angels into Virgins, blessed with a sacred womb. Even without red or pink paint, those colours might stain your dress if you're not careful. Over the next four days, Mother explained menstruation and the precautions to follow. She said the transitional phase, like a pupa, had ended, and I had emerged as a beautiful butterfly. What bothered me more than no longer being called an angel was that my cream-coloured dress, a gift from Sponsor Uncle worn only three times for Sunday Mass, could no longer be worn due to blood stains.

Sponsor Uncle started sending letters along with chocolates, cards and dresses. Though I've never met him, he communicated through these letters. I don't know who he is or where he's from, as Mother didn't provide details. I couldn't reply because Mother forbade it. She would read the letters, mask the postal seal with her pen, then give them to me. I've tried to draw his picture based on details in the letters. I wrote replies on the back of some paintings, but Mother only sent those without writing as thanks.

(*I should be angry about this, but I know she only sent my best pictures, and I avoided writing on those. To be honest, I wasn't that angry.*)

When I asked why I couldn't respond to Sponsor Uncle, Mother said, 'When you turn eighteen, you can leave Santhome. You can seek him out and meet personally. You'll have much to discuss then. Why spoil the fun by telling everything now?'

This made me uneasy, realizing I might have to leave the orphanage as an adult and be responsible for my own life.

You must have noticed the changes in my body and mind as I started menstruating. I don't think it's necessary to detail all that here, as you can read it in a health magazine. What's your opinion? Whatever your response, I'll continue without such physical descriptions. As part of these changes, I began to masturbate. It was as enjoyable as painting a butterfly.

Usually, when I finish a butterfly painting:

1. I would be very happy and satisfied.
2. I would show the picture to Mother.

However, with masturbation:

1. I felt immense guilt.
2. I didn't tell Mother.

Mother's harsh discipline from *Leviticus* intensified my guilt. Isn't it a terrible sin? I felt fear and regret and thought about cutting off my fingers.

I've tried to stop, but my fingers trace invisible pictures against my will. Over time, I realized I wasn't alone, and that lessened my guilt. Some girls at Santhome and schoolmates also do this. We discuss it discreetly. I prefer drawing butterflies on my skin now, making my body a butterfly sanctuary. Though Leviticus scared me, the Song of Solomon eased my guilt and brought pleasure. In dreams, I ride a cedar palanquin carried by Israeli escorts.

Now I understand masturbation isn't a big sin. It helps avoid bigger wrongdoings at my age. At times, riding Solomon's palanquin was my only escape from guilt imposed by Mother's warnings and the Bible. So, I took that ride repeatedly, floating and enjoying the escorts' sweet humming.

You may know that my schoolmates asked me to accompany them to Palika Bazar, where I was introduced into this textbook. Because of warnings given to the women entering Palika alone, my schoolmate asked me to join her. We went there to buy a toy for her. Remember when the Merchant of Palika closely observed my ID card? Two crucial details from that incident were:

- Age: 15
- Blood group: HH

As three girls our age entered Palika Bazar, many peddlers and shop owners watched in amazement. Some met us with sleazy inquiries. The merchant later told me this was typical for that market. However, that trip to Palika turned my life upside down. My friend led me to Electro Hut, and I wanted to escape the obscene atmosphere quickly. The merchant greeted us, asking, 'What do you want to buy, girls?'

My friend didn't answer, and I regretted coming. We tried to distract the merchant by looking at toy cars, watches, CDs and music systems, but no one dared ask for what we actually needed. Even in the air-conditioned shop, I was sweating profusely. The merchant seemed to understand our situation and went inside. He returned with a box and placed dildos and vibrators on the glass table. Seeing these devices, I felt a chill down my spine and started trembling.

The merchant described each item on the table. Some devices, in various colours and shapes, looked like torture tools. As he continued, fear grew inside me. He then brought out the pink butterfly. Although he mentioned its name, I couldn't remember it. The shape and colour attracted me, not the name. It was an expensive Chinese vibrator shaped like a pink butterfly. Instead of imagining a teenager hiding a fluttering butterfly in her panty, picture a girl flying through clouds on a diamond-jewelled butterfly in wonderland.

I woke from a dream hearing, 'My Angel Child...' realizing it was actually a steel toy hitting the glass table. My friend chose a Fetish Die. She was clearly her gambler father's daughter. After purchasing it, we left immediately. As you know, I have a strong affinity for pink and butterflies. I couldn't resist the pink butterfly on the table calling me back.

I returned to the shop, making an excuse to my friends. The Merchant was packing the toys, but the pink butterfly remained on the table. He offered a discount, but it was still too expensive for me. I shared my financial situation and orphanhood, hoping to somehow own it. For a moment, I feared the Merchant might take advantage of me in the dark godown, but those fears didn't materialize.

Contrary to my fears, nothing bad happened. The Merchant was decent and proposed a business deal. I would act as his agent for outside sales, earning a 5 per cent commission on each sale. By accruing the commission, I could eventually own the pink butterfly. He promised to hand over the toys outside Palika Bazar to prevent a girl from entering alone. He included two conditions:

1. The sales items could be used personally if kept hygienic and undamaged.
2. If I cheated him after receiving the equipment, he'd confront me at school or the orphanage.

I accepted the deal and received a package of Ben Wa Balls. I hid it in my school bag and left Palika with my friends.

Selling toys at school wasn't difficult. I found customers through whispers during breaks and overheard jokes. I sold items ranging from ₹1,000 to ₹5,000. The first few devices were sold to girls, but later I sold to boys too. Even smart guys who made homemade toys bought phallus rings. I kept everything strictly business. I was interested in my female customers' experiences after sales. They shared feedback freely since I delivered the toys. Some thought of boyfriends, others fantasized about models and stars, and a few watched porn. Remember my friend who bought the toy from Palika? She uses it while looking at semi-nude models in magazine ads. I told her I had a half-naked model too, not from movies or magazines. She questioned how I could hide such a picture in the orphanage. Her doubt was valid, but I wasn't lying. My model, bruised but compassionate, can be found even on Santhome's walls.

I started enjoying my secret business. However, just as I was fully enjoying it, my commission neared the pink butterfly's price. Selling Lilo, an oval vibrator resembling a sapphire, would let me own it. But everything changed when I first used Lilo. It malfunctioned, making more noise than usual. After everyone slept, I covered myself and started using it. Instead of a mild hum, Lilo screeched, waking a nearby girl. She screamed, bringing Mother to our dormitory. I tried to cover the girl's mouth but failed. The lights came on, and Lilo slipped from my fingers. Both the vibrator and the girl cried non-stop.

Though I was caught red-handed, Mother didn't scold me harshly. She asked me where I got the device. I lied, saying a classmate shared it. Mother warned me to return it and not repeat this. She explained the sin I'd committed, reciting from the Bible. I was told to kneel and pray with a rosary. But once I closed my eyes, I was carried away on Solomon's palanquin, feeling the breeze with myrrh and frankincense fragrances.

My assumption was that Mother wouldn't tell anyone about yesterday's incident. But then, how did the principal summon me to the cabin the next day for allegedly selling sex toys on school premises? Why are the police after me? Am I going to get arrested? Who betrayed me? When I was caught, I had hidden the deceptive sapphire stone in my school bag as a precaution. I can't clearly remember the days that followed. Confused and scared, I moved from place to place, undergoing interrogations.

Here's what I can recall from those doomed days:

1. I was arrested for selling sex toys.
2. I had to visit many places for interrogations.

3. Due to my age, I was bailed out of jail and sent back to the orphanage.
4. Mother informed me that Sponsor Uncle had come to my rescue.
5. Remember the man talking to Mother when I rushed into her room? That was Sponsor Uncle.
6. Sponsor Uncle tried to help me get acquitted from the case.
7. Meanwhile, the Customs Department intercepted an inflatable doll addressed to Santhome Orphanage.
8. Multiple cases were filed against me, landing me in serious trouble.
9. On the eve of the final verdict, my Sponsor Uncle picked me up from Santhome Orphanage. We took a walk through Delhi's busy streets and stayed in a hotel room that evening.
10. Interestingly, I met Sponsor Uncle for the first and last time on Sundays. I had my period on both occasions.
11. The court verdict went against me. I was sentenced to one year in a juvenile home.
12. After the court procedures, on my way to the juvenile home, a constable inexplicably pushed me out of a speeding police vehicle.

Exercise

I. What are the special features of Solomon's palanquin?

Ans:

King Solomon's palanquin, mentioned in the 'Song of Songs', a biblical poem, was built from Lebanese wood. It had silver poles and a gold canopy. Inside the palanquin, the cushions were embroidered with beautiful designs. The mightiest of Israel, sixty warriors skilled in battle, surrounded the palanquin. During his wedding procession, King Solomon rode triumphantly through the streets with his bride beside him, using the palanquin. As the palanquin passed, the people of Jerusalem looked on in wonder, admiring its beauty and the splendour of its occupants. Solomon's palanquin was a symbol of his power and wealth, reflecting the glory of his reign over Israel.

II. Write a poem about the pink butterfly, imagining yourself as the inmate girl at the Santhome orphanage.

Ans:

It gently flutters, flaps its wings,
A sound so soft, the joy it brings.

A magical gadget, a wonder to see,
Free and pink, it sets our spirits free.
With every beat, we feel alive,
A journey deep and so divine.
Our hearts fill up with all its might,
A world of pleasure for all in sight.

III. You may have noticed the title of this chapter. Can you find a children's classic novel related to it and write what would have happened if the Santhome girl had been a character in that novel?

Ans:

The title of this chapter is inspired by Alice in Wonderland. And so, the story begins...

Santhome girl falls down a rabbit hole and enters a fantastical world known as Palika Bazar. She steps through a shop's entrance and meets the Merchant Hatter of Palika Bazar, who wears a top hat and a bow tie. The eccentric Merchant Hatter greets her with a twinkle in his eyes, inviting her to a tea party with seemingly animated sex toys.

Oversized sex toys tower above her on the shelves, beckoning her into a whimsical adventure. Santhome girl's curiosity leads her to a section filled with vibrating toys promising to change her size. She carefully picks up a vibrating wand. As its gentle hum envelops her, she feels herself shrinking. She giggles in delight, looking up at the towering toys, now small enough to explore their world.

Among the towering figures, she meets a talking plush rabbit who guides her through a maze of enchanting aisles and secret paths. As she navigates this mystical place, she finds herself immersed in intimate moments amidst the darkness.

Santhome girl's secret journey through the wonderful toy shop is filled with pleasure and adventure. She experiences the whimsical magic of her surroundings. With the Merchant Hatter, she attends a lively tea party where phallus-shaped teacups dance and sugar cubes sing obscene songs. Using a jigsaw puzzle map of a sleazy picture, she navigates the vast store. She encounters curious puzzles that challenge her wits and vibrant vibrators that dance in sync with her laughter.

Each toy seems to have a story of ecstasy, and she relishes uncovering their secrets. As the sun begins to set, Santhome girl realizes it's time to leave Wonderland. With a heart full of gratitude and memories, she bids farewell to her new-found sex toys and the Merchant Hatter.

With a final playful twist of a vibrating wand, Santhome girl returns to her normal size. She steps back through the *shop's entrance, leaving the magical realm behind. Blinking in the fading daylight, she smiles at the incredible adventure and pleasure she has just experienced in Wonderland.*

IV. Write a short note about the HH blood group, which was mentioned on the ID card of the Santhome girl.

Ans:

The HH blood group, also known as the Bombay blood group, is a rare blood type first discovered in Mumbai, formerly known as Bombay. People with this blood group lack the H antigen in their red blood cells. This absence makes it challenging to type their blood using the standard ABO blood typing system. Individuals with the Bombay blood group can only receive blood from others with the same blood type. This restriction makes it crucial for them to inform their healthcare providers and blood banks about their unique blood type. By sharing this information, people with the Bombay blood group can ensure safe blood transfusions when needed. This awareness is vital for their health and well-being in medical situations requiring blood products.

Hotel

5

One Who Is the Devil and the Deep Blue Sea

In agreement with the news report, what I am saying about my car accident is that...

I am known by different names throughout this story. In Chapter 3, I'm the 'Customs Officer'. Chapter 4 calls me the 'Sponsor Uncle'. Chapter 7 will refer to me as the 'Husband'. Therefore, I am jumping straight into the story as I feel there is no need for any special introduction.

So far, you've only seen my darker side. You know me as the killer who shot the Merchant in Palika Bazar. You've seen me as the man indirectly responsible for the girl's death in Santhome Orphanage. You've witnessed me as the neglectful husband. But there's more to me, like a hidden seabed. This hidden side is usually calm. Sometimes, though, it creates tides and eddies that disturb the surroundings. To fully understand me, you need to know both sides of my personality. Without them, the chapters in this textbook are incomplete. Let's explore this other part of me.

I Who Am the *Husband*

I had a strong, muscular body, but I considered my face and dark complexion unattractive. These were my perceived weaknesses. Despite my good financial status and academic achievements, I struggled to find a girlfriend. It was only towards the end of my college life that I managed to do so. At that point, I became arrogant, shedding all my previous cynicism and inferiority complexes. There were days when I couldn't believe the person in the mirror was actually me. But those false hopes shattered when I realized I was just a temporary fling for her. This made me feel even more unattractive. To escape those gloomy days, I immersed myself in books and prepared for many recruitment exams. Eventually, I joined the Customs Department at twenty-four. It took years of hard work to heal the wounds of love. Although not completely healed, they became like smouldering coal covered in ash, easily stirred by any breeze. They were like a calm seabed, waiting for waves to disrupt it. And that's exactly what happened. Without much choice, I got married after eight monotonous years of work. When mentioning the marriage to others, I often used the excuse that it was at my family's insistence.

At thirty-two, I married a twenty-one-year-old woman. The eleven-year age gap makes me feel inferior, especially because I'm not particularly attractive. It reminds me of my failed past relationship, and her youth exacerbates my feelings of inadequacy. I thought my wife's youth and beauty would compensate for my insecurities, but the truth was that the smouldering coal within me became more exposed with every challenge married life brought.

Early in our marriage, my wife revealed her previous romantic relationship. I tried to comfort her, saying, 'That's all in the past, right? Don't dwell on it too much.'

However, like many men, I felt upset. I learnt that she had agreed to our marriage after enduring emotional abuse from her parents, who had locked her in her bedroom. Despite my comforting words, I couldn't help but wonder, *Do you still love him?*

She skilfully avoided that question, likely fearing any answer would upset me further. As an insecure and pessimistic person, I anticipated uneasy days ahead.

After the marriage, she quickly established her authority over me by eliminating unfamiliarity in the first few days. I still doubt it was a voluntary submission. My daily routines, habits, likes, dislikes and expenses changed drastically. Perhaps the term 'henpecked' suits me now. Realizing she hadn't forgotten her ex-boyfriend fuelled thoughts of revenge against the lover who had abandoned me. That was the first stage of failure.

My sexual relationship with my wife marked the second stage of failure. It never brought me complete fulfilment. I can divide my sex life with my wife into two distinct parts:

1. Before Mastectomy:

You can learn more about my wife's left breast in Chapter 7. I had to engage in intimacy without touching the left breast, as if I were a skilled circus performer. Any accidental contact would have disastrous consequences. In the early days of our marriage, it felt like encountering the sensitive tentacle of a snail. She would curl up in bed, writhing in pain.

As time went by, her reactions became even more intense. It was akin to touching the horn of a charging rhino. She would abruptly jump up, scream and rush into the bathroom. I had to follow her instructions meticulously, behaving like an obedient child. I had to comply with her guidance on where to touch and where to avoid.

This situation was deeply humiliating for me, and she was well aware of it. Despite undergoing numerous medical examinations over the years, the exact cause of her pain remained elusive. Hence, a few years later, when a test revealed a slight suspicion of malignancy, she made the brave decision to undergo immediate surgery to remove her breast, without exploring other treatment options.

2. After Mastectomy:

After her left breast was amputated, the pain subsided, and she was ready to resume a normal sex life. However, things took a turn for the worse. The sight of her naked body without a breast brought to mind a haunting creature known as Ottamulachi, an evil demigoddess with a single breast, and a figure from my grandmother's tales. Ottamulachi, with her dishevelled hair and blood-stained nipple, would howl in the stories.

Suddenly, it felt as though I was the one curling up in bed, seeking refuge like a snail retreating into its shell. I felt suffocated, trapped in that dark and slimy confinement. But eventually, I summoned the courage to shatter that shell and break free. That's why, when I received an official transfer to Delhi, I made the difficult decision to leave my wife behind at our native home and embark on the journey alone.

I Who Am the *Sponsor Uncle*

On a tedious yet busy day in Delhi, I came across a newspaper article about the deaths of my ex-girlfriend and her husband. At that moment, instead of feeling resentment or disappointment, I had a strong desire to finally see her body, something I had once longed for. I met the orphaned girl at the hospital. She was unconscious but had miraculously survived a near-death experience. It remains unclear why the girl's relatives didn't take her in after her parents' deaths and instead handed her over to an orphanage after her recovery. This lingering doubt frequently crossed my mind.

The death of my former lover erased an old grudge but also made my life bleaker. Although I had been married for a few years, we had no children. Hence, I chose to sponsor that girl from Santhome Orphanage, where she had become an inmate. The first time I saw her was when the nun who ran the orphanage introduced her to me while she was playing with other children. I'm certain that the nun never revealed my identity to her. Known as Mother at the orphanage, the nun showered blessings and prayers on me for sponsoring a child.

What I did wasn't necessarily a great act of kindness but rather a response to the feeling that my life lacked curiosity and mystery. It was flowing monotonously without any excitement, so I decided to keep my sponsorship but hide it from my wife.

Although I had sent her many gifts, including chocolates, clothes and greeting cards, I refrained from visiting her at the orphanage. Instead, I remained hidden in the dark comfort of my own cocoon. The nun had mentioned several times that the child was asking to see me or at least asking to be allowed to send letters in reply. However, I didn't respond positively to her requests and gave strict instructions to the nun that the girl should not find my postal addresses in the gifts and letters I sent. Sending her clothes, letters and chocolates became a routine and mindless task for me during my mundane days in Delhi.

After living in Delhi for six years, I was transferred back to Kochi. During my journey back, I had an unexpected encounter with the girl for the second time. I went to Santhome to inform them about my return to my hometown and expressed my desire to continue sponsoring the girl. While speaking with the nun, the girl entered the room. At a glance, I could tell it was her from the startled expression on her face, even before the nun introduced her. After six years, she had undergone significant changes and now resembled her mother. Her face carried a sense of familiarity that I knew I would recognize not just in the Santhome Orphanage but in any crowded corner of the world. The nun interrupted our conversation and shared some good news, 'That little angel has grown into a young woman.'

As I gazed upon the paintings she used to send me, my mind would always travel back to a time when she was just a little girl. It's incredible how fast they grow up. As the colours of her drawings began to fade away, a portrait of my ex-girlfriend at the age of thirteen came to life before my very eyes. She had transformed from a sweet, angelic child into a memory of a past love. In that moment,

Once, when we caught a sex doll from Hong Kong, I summoned the recipient to my office. He looked dishevelled in his loose shirt, jeans, untrimmed beard, and lazy expression. I was in a bad mood that day and interrogated him rudely. He quickly transformed from a serious man to a child about to cry. I asked for his ID to note details before issuing warnings. When I returned his wallet, I noticed an old black-and-white passport-sized photo of my wife smiling.

At that moment, I was more shaken than him. Further questioning revealed he was a journalist, and the woman in the photo was his ex-girlfriend from college. He was still single and depressed eight years after their break-up. I took the photo and tore it into pieces, saying, 'Now she is my wife. So, I'm not interested in seeing her in someone else's wallet. Do you understand?'

Relieved to be out of trouble, he hurried out, nodding in agreement.

I sold the seized sex doll to an agent in Palika Bazar and sent the money to the address in Santhome. This was my way of maintaining sponsorship while avoiding my wife's scrutiny. Through this arrangement, I got to know the agent who regularly supplied such items to Delhi's Palika Bazar. Each time I felt guilty, I tried to make up for it by sending more chocolates, drawing books, watercolours and clothes to the girl in Santhome. I attempted to hide my guilt behind vibrant colours and acts of kindness.

Though deeply unsettling, I didn't reveal to my wife the identity of the person I'd apprehended. Now, I seek solace in myself and the girl from Santhome, using them as an escape from boring subservience to my wife. I remember her face, desperately calling out to the nun, her body strained from running. A vague red stain on her dress lingers in my mind. I kept her drawings on my office desk instead of taking them home, along with the butterflies she depicted. These elements create a Humbertian (signifies self-delusion and moral reprehensibility) hideaway known as the Santhome girl.

For now, she's like a tiny turret, but soon, she'll become a tremendous fortress I'll conquer. I am a patient warrior. By the time she turns eighteen, I'll have to transition from the emptiness of one breast to the fullness of two. Santhome girl is an island where I seek refuge from my tedious failures. Crayon picture flowers and motionless watercolour butterflies will be replaced by real fluttering wings that assist in pollination. There we'll experience only eternal spring, with colours that never fade.

Only the fragrance of love will exist there. However, news of a schoolgirl being arrested for selling toys shattered all these dreams.

The newspaper report didn't shock me. Prior to that, I received a call from a nun in Santhome, who shared some information. The Santhome girl had inadvertently caused the problems. The nun had discovered the girl masturbating with a vibrator two days before that. The girl said a classmate had given it to her. The nun, emphasizing moral values, advised the girl and helped her seek repentance. As the guardian of an orphan girl, the nun informed the school principal about the classmate who had given her the vibrator. She also emphasized the need to prevent such situations from occurring again.

The family of the girl who allegedly received the vibrator learnt about the incident through the school principal. During interrogations, the accused girl revealed that the Santhome girl was selling toys in the school and had promised her the vibrator. The principal tried to conceal this to protect the school's reputation. However, after receiving a complaint from the accused girl's parents, the police initiated a case, leading to the newspaper report.

Given the sensitive nature of the case, the nun informed me that the church couldn't intervene on Santhome's behalf. I used my official position to make arrangements in Delhi. I appointed a competent criminal lawyer for the girl and prepared for her bail. When the case hearing began, I took an extended leave and returned to Delhi. Although I didn't meet her in person, I provided all the necessary assistance and observed the court proceedings.

To help the girl's case, the lawyer proposed involving a sexologist during the trial. The sexologist presented several arguments to the court:

A. In a country like India, where sexually transmitted diseases like HIV are prevalent, promoting safe sex methods is crucial.
B. Not all individuals who use such devices are mentally ill.
C. Sex toys are helpful for physically challenged people, those with difficulty achieving orgasm, those experiencing delayed ejaculation and those with other sexual disorders.
D. Sex toys provide a safer alternative for individuals who engage in unsafe sexual practices.

Despite these arguments, the court rejected them under the provisions of the Indian Penal Code.

The girl's lawyer was astute in not disclosing the business relationship between the Merchant of Palika and the Santhome girl during the trial. Additional points considered were:

A. The girl is a teenager residing in an orphanage.
B. Adolescent agility is often misunderstood as juvenile delinquency.
C. Though she may have had the device, it was for personal use, not for sale.

It seemed likely that these arguments would lead to the girl's acquittal. She was almost safe, except that if found guilty, her current suspension from school could result in expulsion. The nun assured me she could stay in the orphanage until the verdict.

Everything fell apart just a week before the final verdict. Customs inspection intercepted a parcel containing a sex doll addressed to the Santhome girl. This development completely altered the case. The new evidence undermined arguments suggesting the girl only used sex devices for personal purposes. The seized inflatable sex doll, explicitly designed for men, strongly indicated her involvement in selling sex toys at school. The lawyer acknowledged that given these new circumstances, the verdict would likely be unfavourable, potentially leading to imprisonment. I found myself in a situation where any hope of a positive outcome was rapidly fading, like a sinking Humbertian hideaway.

Ah, what a paradox indeed!

- For nearly nine years, I've protected that girl through sponsorship.
- The money for sponsorship came from selling sex toys.
- Yet, those same toys have become a curse in her life.
- I wonder what awaits her at the juvenile home.
- I've heard rumours about underage sex workers and their rackets.
- It's hard to imagine a sweet teenage girl ending up there.

I'm certain pink butterflies will never take flight from her fingers again. Instead, they'll curl up inside the chrysalis like a snail in a spiral shell. They'll suffer a slow, languishing death in a dark, colourless world, confined within a self-made cage. With her, I lost the life I had envisioned, one that could have liberated me from my persistent setbacks.

I took the girl from Santhome on the eve of the final judgment. When I told the nun I'd personally bring her to court the next day, she agreed, allowing the girl some relief from the dull wait. We spent the evening exploring Delhi's bustling streets. Though she'd lived in Delhi long, she had gone to the orphanage at age seven and was forbidden to roam outside. Many things were new to her. We ended our stroll in the evening and reached my lodge room.

The receptionist who handed over the key must have mistaken her for a call girl, giving me the usual welcome and smile. Perhaps he didn't misunderstand because she carried a school bag full of clothes instead of a vanity bag, an extra body part for call girls. I reached the room without worrying about his thoughts. The room was non-air-conditioned with average amenities.

That day she realized I was her Sponsor Uncle. The excitement must have lessened her fear of the impending judgment. Until then, I'd avoided asking about the case or sex toys, knowing it would upset her. However, after settling into the room, she began to confess. She spoke of colour palettes, pink butterflies, the mother of Santhome who adored angels, the fat Merchant of Palika Bazar and the pink butterfly vibrator awaiting her... She concluded with surprising maturity, leaving me with many unanswered questions.

I lit a cigarette and began telling the story of Humbert and Lolita like my grandmother's tales, trying to soothe her restless mind. After dinner, we settled on the bed. By the end of the story, she was drenched in sweat. She went to shower before bed. Remarkably, I transformed from storyteller to Humbert himself. Peeking through the bathroom door gap, I realized it had been long since I'd seen a naked body with two breasts. I felt slightly panicked.

'You know... Lolita and her stepfather Humbert end up sleeping in a bed in a similar hotel room named Enchanted Hunters during a trip. That's when they have sex for the first time.'

I never thought I could present this so effortlessly. My purpose became clear to her. Expecting rejection, she quickly changed the subject.

'Will the court punish me? Tell me, Uncle... Do I have to go to prison?'

'Let's believe the court won't punish you. Even if they do, there's another law outside. Don't think everything ends with one judgment. I assure you, you won't rot in a prison cell.'

She began to cry. As Humbert, my gaze locked onto her lowered eyes. Like a dog, I sniffed Lolita's dress. Each part of her body elicited different sensations. The smell of menstrual blood disappointed me. I was constantly confronted with defeat... Victory seemed out of reach. She sensed my withdrawal. I found comfort in my failures' ashes. Despite that, she lay down exhausted, seeking solace in my presence. Even as a teenager, she must have realized that being with a man relinquishing his sexual desires is like sitting next to a Zen monk.

The court verdict was against the girl. She was sentenced to eighteen months in a juvenile home. The magistrate stated he initially thought a strict warning would suffice but couldn't overlook a teenage girl obtaining these items from abroad for resale. To discover the foreign package's origin, I bribed a court clerk. Once I had the information, I asked colleagues to check for previous deliveries from the same Hong Kong address and to see if it was blacklisted. I also tasked my Delhi agent to find the source of the girl's sex toys. He shared important information about her connection with Palika Bazar.

I had promised the Santhome girl that I wouldn't send her to prison. I had to keep my word. That's why I approached the police constable escorting her from the court to the juvenile home. I offered him a hefty bribe, paying half in advance. His task was simple. He had to ensure that my promise was kept. Something had to happen during the journey to prevent her enrolment in the juvenile home. As she was taken away in a police vehicle after the court proceedings, she frantically looked around for someone. Unable to face her, I hid in the court crowd. If the escort policeman was to be believed, this would be the last time I'd see her alive. I felt as if the last piece of land beneath my feet had submerged. I didn't know who to blame for these events, but I had two leads: a location in Kochi where a previous delivery from the same Hong Kong address had occurred and a mention of a fat Merchant from Palika Bazar.

After booking a flight to my hometown, I vacated my lodge room. On my way to Palika Bazar with a travel bag, I confirmed I was carrying a Beretta-type handgun bought from the black market a week ago. Entering Palika Bazar, I felt as if all the displayed items had arrived through my agent, making me the evil source of all obscenity in that place. As I walked towards a shop called Electro Hut, owned by a fat Merchant, I received a phone call from Kochi. The caller informed me that my wife had been involved in an accident and hadn't survived and had passed away a few minutes ago. At that moment, everything slipped out of my control.

I Who Am the *Music Lover*

I felt like Professor Humbert when he sought revenge on Clare Quilty for separating him from Lolita. Metallica's 'Enter Sandman' played in the shop. Once a favourite, I now despised it. The Merchant sat at the cash counter, counting money and humming, 'Exit light... Enter night...' In a hallucination, I imagined him naked like Quilty at the piano. Suddenly, he noticed me and turned to face me.

When I asked for The Beatles album with 'Lucy in the Sky with Diamonds,' he said business was over. However, he became obedient when I showed him my department ID. He found the album and played it at my instruction. I closed my eyes, enjoying the music, my finger tapping the gun's trigger to the beat.

'This is my favourite song, sir. Don't some songs make you feel like you've died when they end? It's one of those... "Lucy in the Sky with Diamonds".'

'Did you know there was a girl who painted as well as Lucy's Julian? And another man who dreamed she was flying through the sky wearing a jewelled crown.'

I led the Merchant of Palika to the godown at gunpoint. Pressing him against the wall, I put the gun in his mouth. Suddenly, I could feel his erect penis touching my body, and I shot him without a second thought. I had gone to Palika Bazar with the intention of killing the Merchant, but I wasn't entirely sure if I would follow through. Perhaps I would give him a scary warning or treat him like a punching bag, and then, just maybe, I would eventually return. However, my fingers acted reflexively as I found myself in a state of lewdness. As his head split, red streaks spread across the wall. Butterflies danced on the sky-blue walls to 'Lucy in the Sky...' I wiped my fingerprints carefully and placed the gun in his lifeless hand.

After leaving the godown, I took the album out of the music system, placed it in my bag, and then randomly selected a CD from the table to insert into the music system. As the Backstreet Boys' 'I Want It That Way' played, I left, singing along...

Believe when I say
I want it that way
But we are two worlds apart
Can't reach to your heart...

While waiting to board the flight, my mobile rang, and it was a call from a colleague. He informed me that a recipient in Kochi had received a similar parcel that had arrived earlier from Hong Kong – a case I had handled, according to official records. Upon receiving the address over an SMS, I recalled the person associated with it – the journalist who had kept my wife's old photo in his wallet. The old case records mentioned the same type of sex doll that had been sent to the girl in Santhome. I quickly texted the address to a couple of my friends in the police, asking them to do a background check. After boarding the flight, I switched off my mobile phone and closed my eyes for a while.

The accidental death of my ex-girlfriend and her husband...

The recent death of my wife, whose body is still in the mortuary...

The death of the Merchant of Palika in a godown...

The possible death of the Santhome girl that may have occurred during that time...

A ballet of deaths intertwined and holding hands together...

My colleague was waiting for me when I got off the flight. He was on duty at the airport that day. I borrowed his bike and began riding towards the mortuary. Halfway there, I received a call from a police friend. He informed me that they had searched the address I provided earlier. The results were unexpected. The person wasn't just involved in the illegal sex toy trade. He was also a Maoist militant who had been killed in an encounter. This news piqued my interest. I was now more eager to see the journalist who had been shot than I was to receive my wife's body.

I decided to take a detour to the journalist's house. Despite the mental turmoil caused by the recent deaths, I rode the bike with proper caution as usual. But suddenly, a car collided with me from behind. The impact was jarring, and I felt a surge of pain course through my body. My mind raced with thoughts of the case, the journalist and the unexpected turn of events. But now, I had a more immediate concern to deal with.

Ouch! That was... Argh!... a car... and it's coming back... Oh! No... no...

Exercise

I. You may have noticed that this lesson mentions three music bands: The Beatles, Metallica and Backstreet Boys.
Write a brief note about their performances and particularities.

Ans:

The Beatles, Metallica and Backstreet Boys: all boast massive global fan bases. Each has achieved great success with multiple albums and numerous awards. These bands emerged in different eras: The Beatles in the 1960s, Metallica in the 1980s and the Backstreet Boys in the 1990s. Each carved out their own unique musical path.

The Beatles thrived as a rock band, Metallica as a heavy metal powerhouse and Backstreet Boys as a prominent pop group. Their songwriting approaches differed significantly. The Beatles primarily relied on John Lennon and Paul McCartney's talents, crafting compositions with poetic and introspective lyrics. Metallica collaborated as a group, exploring darker themes like death, war and personal struggles. The Backstreet Boys worked with separate songwriters, often focusing on love, relationships and personal experiences.

Live performances also set these bands apart. The

Beatles were renowned for their vibrant and energetic live performances. Metallica's shows were characterized by their intense stage presence and heavy sonic assault.The Backstreet Boys' performances frequently incorporated choreographed dance routines and interactive audience engagement, both in their video albums and live shows.

II. Jot down any five famous quotes about the power and impact of music.

Ans:

1. 'Music is the shorthand of emotion.' – Leo Tolstoy
2. 'Without music, life would be a mistake.' – Friedrich Nietzsche
3. 'Music expresses that which cannot be put into words.' – Victor Hugo
4. 'Music is the art which is most nigh to tears and memories.' – Oscar Wilde
5. 'Music is a moral law. It gives soul to the universe and wings to the mind.' – Plato

III. Do you think there is any chance for ifs and buts in the jigsaw puzzle of deaths mentioned in this chapter? If so, what are they?

Ans:

1. *The Santhome girl's fate might have been different if circumstances in the lodge room had been different. Perhaps if she hadn't been menstruating, or if she and the customs officer had become intimate, events might have unfolded differently.*
2. *The Merchant of Palika's death could have been avoided under different circumstances. If the customs officer hadn't known about his wife's death just before entering Palika Bazar, or if he had not had an erection when threatened with a gun in his mouth, the outcome might have been different. The customs officer, caught in that awkward predicament, fired a shot almost instinctively, his finger pulling the trigger without conscious thought.*
3. *The journalist's friend's death in the encounter might have been prevented with better timing. If the customs officer had discovered the connection between the journalist and the Hong Kong address earlier, and if the police had received this information sooner, perhaps the situation could have been resolved differently.*

IV. What is the trivia behind the reference to Julian and The Beatles song 'Lucy in the Sky with Diamonds' in this chapter?

Ans:

'Lucy in the Sky with Diamonds' is a song by The Beatles that appeared on their 1967 album 'Sgt. Pepper's Lonely Hearts Club Band'. It is one of their most popular and memorable songs. John Lennon and Paul McCartney wrote it. The song's title came from a picture that Julian, John Lennon's son, drew of a girl named Lucy. Some people think that the song is about the drug LSD because the title has the letters 'LSD' in it. But John Lennon and Paul McCartney say that the song is not about drugs and that the title was derived from Julian's drawing. The lyrics drew inspiration from Alice in Wonderland and the surreal imagery prevalent in Lewis Carroll's literary works.

Julian was three years old when he drew the picture of Lucy O'Donnell, who was in his nursery school class. John Lennon saw the picture and liked it, which led to the creation of the song. Julian was also known as 'Jules', and Paul McCartney wrote a song called 'Hey Jules' to comfort Julian during his parents' divorce. Later, they changed the name of the song to 'Hey Jude', and it became one of The Beatles' most famous songs. Julian Lennon had a complicated relationship with his father. He was not mentioned in John Lennon's will, which caused legal disagreements, and a settlement was eventually reached.

V. You might have observed that the title of this chapter includes an idiom. Can you explain how it originated?

Ans:

The idiom 'between the devil and the deep blue sea' is an expression used to describe a difficult or challenging situation where one is faced with two equally undesirable choices. It implies being caught between two unfavourable options and having to make a decision without a clear or satisfactory outcome.

The origin of this idiom is somewhat uncertain, with several theories proposed to explain its roots. One theory suggests that the phrase originated from nautical terminology during the Age of Sail. In this context, 'the devil' referred to the seam between the deck planking and the ship's side, which was considered a dangerous and hard-to-reach area to work on. 'The deep blue sea' referred to the ocean itself, representing the perils and uncertainties of sailing. Sailors who found themselves working in the difficult space between the deck and the side of the ship faced a treacherous situation, hence the idiom.

Another theory suggests that the idiom has religious origins. In Christian theology, the devil is often associated with evil and temptation, while the deep blue sea symbolizes danger or chaos. Biblical stories, such as the story of Jesus walking on water or the story of Jonah and the whale, may have inspired the phrase. These stories depict individuals facing perilous situations where they have to make difficult choices.

The expression most likely emerged from a combination of nautical and religious influences, and over time, it has become a commonly used phrase to describe challenging situations with no easy way out.

Before the advent of GPS navigation apps on smartphones,

a time when people relied solely on paper maps and road atlases

and sought guidance from strangers on street corners for directions...

6

The Survivor

The dead have already shared their own stories, contradicting the newspaper reports. I initially stepped back, intending to prioritize their accounts. But this decision unexpectedly complicated my storytelling. I can't wait any longer. As a living narrator, I don't expect the same level of tolerance you've shown the deceased. While their versions differ, one thing is clear: the news about their lives and deaths differs significantly from the news reports mentioned in Chapter 1.

You need to know the full story. But don't worry, I'm only adding to and clarifying the tales the dead have already told. You may have heard various personal versions as well. So, I'll do my best to avoid repetition. As the living remnant of this puzzle of deaths, I never imagined becoming a chapter in this textbook.

The customs officer's statement about his 'accidental death' drew my attention to this book. Yes, what you are thinking is correct. It was not an accidental death.

I am trying to separate the different phases of the story, leaving aside the techniques regularly used in storytelling.

1. I'll clap loudly to grab your attention.
2. I'll ask you some questions that will require you to think and answer.
3. I'm introducing a *Brain Break* in our session by incorporating the two steps mentioned above.
4. After that break, you can return to the story with a fresh mind.

I was a dreamer, deeply immersed in love and poetry, leading a life that was equal parts romantic and melancholic.

- Oops! I have condensed my entire life so far into a single sentence.
- A period filled with all the energy of life is encapsulated within this sentence.
- It is this same period that I am about to unveil before you.

- You can read my five-year-long love story within this single sentence.
- From the same sentence, you can also understand that I was devastated after the love failure.
- Beyond love and desperation, all that remains in my life is a series of seemingly inconsequential days.
- I don't really remember what I read, what I did, or what I ate or drank during those days.
- If I want to, I can conclude this story and exit this book with this single sentence.
- Didn't I mention that there should be some additions to the stories told by others?
- It is for this reason that I am continuing for now.
- When those additions are nearly finished, I will slowly escape from this story and its premises and disappear.

Brain Break: *I'm going to ask you some questions after clapping my hands five times.*

1. 👏 *2.* 👏 *3.* 👏 *4.* 👏 *5.* 👏

{

 # Who is the poet who came to India from a Pakistani province during the Partition and fell in love with the famous poet Sahir Ludhianvi

and revealed in her autobiography that she used to collect his cigarette butts?

Ans: Amrita Pritam

 # Who is the Canadian poet and singer labelled as 'the poet laureate of pessimism,' 'the grocer of despair,' 'the godfather of gloom' and 'the high priest of pathos' by critics?

Ans: Leonard Cohen

 # Whose poetry contributed to giving a voice to the struggles of the Palestinian people, and who faced multiple imprisonments for his political activism and for publicly reading his poetry?

Ans: Mahmoud Darwish

}

Our love was gentle and inspiring. She was the muse for all the poems I wrote during my college days. Her form, her appearance and even her silly wit fuelled my creativity. Without her, I might have never become a poet. I didn't write any poems before meeting her, and after we broke up, the inspiration faded away. She herself was poetry. The sweat glistening on her skin as she walked in the sun, hands folded, carried the same scent as the droplets of Chelpark ink spreading on white paper while I wrote poems.

Ours wasn't a short-lived romance; we had been in love for a solid five years. As our college days neared their end, we were on the verge of marriage. I had already gained recognition as a young poet. My ambition was to pursue linguistic studies and research. However, everything changed when I decided to marry her. My focus shifted towards securing a job after graduation. Together, we meticulously planned our future. After the final exams, we parted ways, setting a specific place, time and interval to meet again.

Physical interactions had no place in our romance until then. However, on the last day of college, I invited her to the library. There, I embraced her and kissed her on the left breast. That kiss marked the end of the romantic phase of my single-sentence life. After we left college, there was no response from her. When I went to meet her a month later, I learnt that her house had been sold and the family had moved. I searched for her for a long time but couldn't find her. My life of sloth gradually turned me into a drunkard. The memory of her remained with me in the form of a black-and-white passport-sized photo that I kept in my bifold wallet.

What could have happened to her?

- Could she have betrayed me? No, I don't think so.
- Would her family have forced her into an arranged marriage? Hey, I hope not.
- Did she die from illness or in an accident? Oh no! Please, let that not be the case.

Brain Break: *I'm going to ask you some questions after clapping my hands five times.*

1. 👏 *2.* 👏 *3.* 👏 *4.* 👏 *5.* 👏

{

Find out who the poet is after reading the following verses.

 # 1

She loved me, sometimes I loved her.
How could I not have loved her large, still eyes?
I can write the saddest poem of all tonight.
To think I don't have her. To feel that I've lost her.

Ans: Pablo Neruda

 # 2

Who said that memory is a fragrant window
opening on ripe cornfields?
That our bodies grow cold
as the sun grows dim there?

Ans: Koyamparambath Satchidanandan

 # 3

Tired of all who come with words, words but no language
I went to the snow-covered island.
The wild does not have words.
The unwritten pages spread themselves out in all directions!

Ans: Tomas Tranströmer

}

In the days of desperation and laziness following my failed love, I decided to abandon my desire for higher studies. The sudden financial crisis after my father's death shattered my long-nurtured passion for linguistic studies. This forced me into a survival situation where I needed to find a job quickly. I completed a short-term diploma course in journalism and began my journey as a newspaper reporter. Though I carried the title 'journalist', the work was undoubtedly exhausting. I had experienced so many challenging days that I no longer recognized boredom. Nevertheless, the monotonous repetition eventually wore me down. Somehow, I managed to hold onto my profession by writing mundane news reports.

From being a field reporter, I was promoted to the news desk. But due to my sedentary lifestyle, I decided to gradually distance myself from society and my surroundings. After some time, I grew tired of my office desk and fixed-shift schedules. That's when I decided to become an independent journalist. In a way, it made me even lazier. I would crawl like the tortoise in *Aesop's Fables* only when I needed money. Otherwise, I would be as lethargic as the lazy hare that napped under the tree – reading, smoking or lost in thoughts. Somewhere along that challenging journey, the lazy notion of taking shortcuts must have led me astray from the path of the Buddha and onto the path of Angulimala, a notorious bandit who later reformed and became a Buddhist monk. By breaking the cadre law, I am openly acknowledging that I am a Maoist supporter.

Brain Break: *I'm going to ask you some questions after clapping my hands five times.*

1. 👏 *2.* 👏 *3.* 👏 *4.* 👏 *5.* 👏

{

 # From which Indian village is the term 'Naxalite' derived?

Ans: Naxalbari (in West Bengal)

 # What was the slogan that arose during the left-wing peasants' uprising in Naxalbari?

Ans: Land to Tiller

In which year did the Naxalites attack the police station at Thalassery and the police camp at Pulpally in the state of Kerala?

Ans: 1968

Who is the female militant activist who participated in the Pulpally Naxalite action, parted ways with the armed struggle movement and later became a human rights activist in Kerala?

Ans: Kunnikkal Ajitha

 # In which country did the Maoist movement come to power through elections for the first time in history?

Ans: Nepal

}

My involvement in the Naxal movement remains somewhat unclear to me. Looking back, it seems to have offered an escape from a life of laziness and purposelessness. I was drawn to a philosophy focused on class struggle against the state. Perhaps there was always a hidden inclination towards excessive romanticism within me. Actions against the state require adequate logistics and preparation. In south India, however, only fragmented factions and groups were present. Over time, members who embraced a more democratic approach abandoned the ideology and joined other socialist organizations. While I don't fully endorse the belief that militant activism or armed revolution can solve social issues, I do think there should be a force to stand against injustice. Don't you agree? Sometimes, the state would exploit us to feign fulfilling its responsibility to protect its own people.

'Somebody is trying to attack you, and it is the duty of the state to protect you.'

The state establishes its relationship with citizens based on this slogan, this very foundation of fear. Actual or staged encounters often occur as experiments to validate this equation. When rivalries between countries escalate into aggression, people are forced to become refugees. They are often unable to escape their own land and obtain refugee status, thus distorting the state's democratic values. How can we justify the inconsistency of justice that excludes people from their own habitat? The land itself becomes more of an illusion while the sky transforms into a solid surface to walk on. However, I am not inclined to step on it or adhere to such a philosophy. Gradually, I am shifting from the politics of romantic anarchism towards pragmatism and practicality.

***Brain Break:** I'm going to ask you some questions after clapping my hands five times out loud.*

1. 👏 *2.* 👏 *3.* 👏 *4.* 👏 *5.* 👏

{

 # What is 'Apadravya' mentioned in the Kama Sutra, the ancient Indian guide to sexuality?

Ans: Apadravya refers to prosthetic devices used to increase penis size during intercourse, as described in the Kama Sutra.

 # What is Dakimakura?

Ans: Dakimakura is a Japanese term for a large pillow that can be hugged like a body pillow. Dakimakuras often feature pillow covers with Manga or Anime characters in suggestive or erotic poses or outfits.

 # What compound is added to latex to increase the stability and viscosity of sex dolls?

Ans: Zinc Oxide

}

I had nearly distanced myself from the Naxal movement. Life carried on as a string of unfulfilled days. My solitary existence had put me in a challenging position. I wasn't emotionally prepared to pursue or have a partner. Natural desires were misleading me. The pain of past failed love pushed me away from women, yet I couldn't escape my sexual urges. Memories of betrayal left me mentally exhausted, making it impossible to even contemplate seeking the company of prostitutes. Artificial sex toys became the only option for potential satisfaction, though it wasn't a conscious decision.

During a friendly exchange of letters, my friend in Hong Kong mentioned sex dolls. It was through him that I first learned about inflatable dolls. He described them as having flirty eyes, chestnut-coloured hair and open mouths, seemingly ready for intimate acts. I wondered how they would look. Would they have silky, smooth skin, blue crystal eyes, fake yet sharp eyelashes, pink, puffy lips and throbbing latex nipples?

I imagined gazing at such a doll in the darkness, illuminated only by the faint glow of a candle, gently caressing it with my fingers. In my mind, it would withdraw its hand in shame, a result of its cheapness and lack of polish. But I would dance with it (or her). Instead of the typical sounds of breaths and squeals, latex gurgles and plastic grunts would emanate from it. After reaching a climax, I would have to release the air, and it would curl up. I pictured cleansing the synthetic mouth and genitals with soapy bubbles before it peacefully fell asleep.

Brain-Break: *I'm clapping my hands five times out loud.*

1. 👏 *2.* 👏 *3.* 👏 *4.* 👏 *5.* 👏

{

There are no questions this time.
If you want, you can move to another nearby location from your current place and sit there.
Oh, don't be so lazy! Just do it and feel the difference while you continue reading.

}

My friend had written to inform me that he had sent me a sex doll from Hong Kong. But unfortunately,

I couldn't receive it. That bloody customs officer interpreted the rules with a threatening tone and took the doll away from me. He then snatched the photograph from my wallet and tore it up, destroying the remaining memories of my single-sentence life. I was on the verge of tears, like a child who had lost his favourite toy. For the first time, I thought about killing him in that interrogation room. This thought would return to me later, but at that moment, in that interrogation room, I was in a hurry to escape the customs legal hassles.

After losing the photograph, I decided to see her in person to refresh my memory of her face. The only way to find her was to track the customs officer. I used my work breaks to keep an eye on him. During one such observation at the post office, I found a Delhi address on a money order form. He had carelessly discarded it due to a filing error. I didn't know who the woman was or her relationship with the customs officer. However, the note and the amount on the form indicated a very close connection. I saw this as an opportunity to use against him. I wrote a letter to my friend in Hong Kong. In it, I insisted that he send another sex doll, but this time to the address of an orphanage in Delhi. I wasn't sure if he would comply with my request again. However, I believe he did send it. To this day, I don't know what happened to that doll.

When I found my ex-lover at the customs officer's house, I began to relive my single-sentence life. She hadn't betrayed me; her family had forced her into the marriage. Along with my love, she had lost her left breast, which I had once kissed. Despite the amputation, my love remained imprinted on the remnants of the scar. I would meet her whenever I had the opportunity and the customs officer was away. But I had no intention of becoming a typical friend with benefits. She promised to leave her unhappy family life and join me. But once again, I lost her. Just before she died, she pleaded to me, asking me not to wait for her any longer. At that moment, I thought she was planning to continue her married life with the customs officer. I had no idea she was about to take her own life.

Her death from falling from the third floor of the house... I still can't believe it was accidental. That evening, I sat in my room, unsure of what to do after hearing the news of her death. My friend from Hong Kong called to inform me he was coming to meet me in person. I was numb and not in the mood to respond. I didn't even ask him to cancel his visit. Even though I had met him after many years, I still couldn't get her death out of my mind.

I wanted to see her body one last time before the burial. I lied to my friend, saying, 'I need to urgently see a friend.' He handed me the key to his car and asked me to return quickly. As I drove out of the house, I saw a herd of cattle grazing by the roadside. They were an obstacle. Startled by the car's horn, they rushed into the marshy area across from them.

Coincidences... Do they happen as surprises? Why else would I see the customs officer coming from the opposite direction while I was driving to see her dead body? Without any hesitation, I hit him with the car. Like the scattered pieces of a black-and-white passport photo, he had torn off once before, his bike and body were flung into the air. To confirm that he was dead, I reversed the vehicle and ran over his body once more. After that, I continued my journey to see another corpse, leaving one behind on the road.

As I mentioned at the beginning of this chapter, I have tried to clarify some ambiguities. Now it's time for me to exit this book and disappear from this story... Bye!

Exercise

I. Do you think that the person referred to as the 'survivor' in this chapter, who has committed crimes, including murder, is likely to be caught? Please provide the reasons.

Ans:

The 'survivor' has a very low chance of being caught.

1. *The car used in the murder doesn't belong to him but to a friend.*
2. *The friend who could have provided information about him was killed in a staged encounter.*
3. *The story is set before 2010, when CCTV cameras and other tracking systems were scarce.*
4. *Even if he avoids prison for his crime, he might end up living a lonely, scared and dull life.*
5. *So, there doesn't seem to be much difference between such a life and imprisonment.*

II. What are 'brain breaks' in the education field?

Ans:

Brain breaks in education are short, structured pauses incorporated into the classroom routine. They help students restore focus, alleviate stress and enhance learning. These breaks involve activities that engage students in physical movement, mindfulness exercises or brief periods of rest. The purpose is to provide students with a mental reset. This allows their brains to recharge and optimize cognitive functioning.

Research suggests that incorporating brain breaks into the classroom can have several positive effects on students. These include reducing stress, increasing productivity, boosting brain function and developing social skills. The implementation of brain breaks has resulted in increased student engagement.

III. Write a brief note about sex dolls.

Ans:

Sex dolls are a category that includes sex toys with a female body shape and genitals. It is believed that sex dolls were first used by ancient sailors. The French term 'dame de voyage' refers to cloth dolls that were made by sailors to keep them company during their long voyages at sea. Sex dolls can be made in various forms, which can be rigid or inflated, based on the raw materials used, such as plastic, latex or vinyl. The price of sex dolls varies, depending on factors such as the material, manufacturing process and shape of the final product. Latex dolls that closely resemble the human body have a higher price, while silicone, vinyl or plastic dolls are comparatively less expensive.

IV. What are the sections of the Indian Penal Code that can be used if a case is brought against you regarding the sale and use of toys?

Ans:

Sections 292, 293 and 294 deal with obscenity under the Indian Penal Code. Section 292 states that the publication, sale or distribution of obscene books, pamphlets, papers, writings, drawings, paintings or any other objects is prohibited. Section 293 extends this prohibition to the advertisement or display of such obscene materials, including through audio or visual means. Section 294 deals with obscene acts and songs in public places. It prohibits the utterance, singing, recitation or performance of any obscene words, songs or acts in or near a public place that may cause annoyance to others.

These sections aim to maintain public decency and prevent the dissemination of obscene materials or offensive acts that may be harmful or offensive to society. Violations of these sections may result in legal consequences, such as fines or imprisonment, as determined by the court based on the severity of the offence. But these sections do not explicitly mention religious symbols, idols or sculptures. One possible reason is that these symbolic icons represent the divine and are not intended to be obscene. Another reason may be that religious art and architecture in India often carry symbolic meanings that go beyond their literal or physical aspects.

Once upon a time,

Before Instagram became a sensation...

While Orkut was losing its shine and Facebook was gaining attraction...

When Tarana Burke coined the term 'Me Too' on MySpace[5]*, to unite survivors...*

[5] A social networking website

7

Lilith

Contrary to what the news might say, I am confessing to you about my suicide...

I am not sharing my story while alive, nor after my death...

These revelations are being made in my dying moments...

Now, I'm a Pall, Draped over the Coffin...

What you see now is me, a 31-year-old woman, stepping into the air to jump from a height of 31 feet.

I'm about to jump down from the top of the three-storey house.

The height of one floor	= 10 feet
Total height	= 3 × 10 = 30 feet

I am at this approximate height considering two factors. First, the building's foundation stands slightly above ground level. Second, there's a small parapet on the third floor, let's assume it is one foot. Together, these elements contribute to the total height of 31 feet.

Do you know that Neil Armstrong declared, '*That's one small step for a man, one giant leap for mankind,*' as he stepped on the moon?

My life unfolds like a book as I fall through the air. My body accelerates following the laws of motion. I'll pass the second floor faster than the 10-foot distance of the top floor. The ground floor will rush by even quicker than the other two. This dynamic shift might affect how I narrate my story. As my brain shatters from the fall, the moments and incidents in my story may also fragment. Falling upside down, the chronology of my tale will be in reverse order. I ask you to keep up with the speed of my fall and the scattered nature of my narration.

These are the methods I use to overcome my fear of jumping by looking down and calculating the height:

A. To escape my body's restlessness, I imagine myself falling to the ground like a cloth hung on a terrace to dry.

B. Gradually, I transform into different clothes falling from the terrace in the wind.
C. Although it's a short journey, I re-read the book of my life to avoid boredom.
D. You can see my life's book as a diary inscribed with famous quotes and sayings. But I'll only share a few pages with you.
E. Your reading will progress from the last page to the first, like a countdown at a rocket launch centre.

Now, I'm a Sexy Satin Nightgown...

- I'm committing suicide.
- My last journey begins.
- The height from the ground is about 31 feet

Albert Camus enunciates in my diary, *'There is only one really serious philosophical problem, and that is suicide.'*

Although the thought of suicide is distressing, I have decided to attempt it in a way that remains unknown to the outside world. I'm staging a scene that appears as if I fell from the third floor while hanging clothes to dry. This includes a bucket of washed clothes, spilled soapy water, clothes stretched out for drying, dress hangers and clothes pegs. My intention is to make it seem like an unfortunate accident caused by slipping on a wet surface. As corroborating evidence, I've deliberately damaged the dryer part of the washing machine. Thus, I intentionally slip from the terrace and fall.

Why am I committing suicide?

Until now, I believed suicide was a last resort, chosen when all options were exhausted. However, the confusion surrounding my choices is pushing me towards it.

A. I've found a lover whom I had lost for years, and I now recognize the warmth of love again. I feel compelled to leave my husband and live with her.
B. My lesbian partner, whom I believed had been lost for months, has reached out to me. Our relationship was so close that we understood each other intimately. I cannot refuse her invitation.
C. I'm considering death as an option; otherwise, I have to continue in my unhappy marriage as long as I remain confused about choosing between options A and B.

On the exact day I had planned to leave my husband and begin a new journey with my old flame from college, I received a call from her. She explained her unexpected departure from the city and expressed her desire to discuss the details in person. During that lengthy phone conversation, she asked me to live with her. How could I possibly resist such an invitation? Wasn't it what I had been eagerly waiting for?

Hours before she called, my lover, the journalist, came home unexpectedly. Initially, I thought it was just a routine visit, but he surprised me.

'You can leave your husband and start a new life in a distant place,' he assured me.

I asked, filled with curiosity, 'Is there really a place called "Far Away"?'

He responded with a reassuring smile, 'Not just one; there are many such places.'

With his words echoing in my mind, I decided to leave everything behind and embark on this new journey with him. We agreed to leave behind all that had happened since our college days and start afresh.

However, after receiving her call, doubt and confusion crept into my mind like a crucial move on a chessboard.

It's a stalemate, what to do?
Tell my dear Bishop and Queen.
Whom to love, him or her?
Torn hearts, him or her?
Damn dilemma, him or her?
Choose wisely, him or her?

I became aware of the potential risks involved, realizing that even the smallest misstep in choosing the next move could profoundly impact the rest of my life

Now, I am a Graffiti Printed T-shirt...

- Height from ground about 30 feet

Agatha Christie whispers in my diary, *'Love can be a very frightening thing. That is why most great love stories are tragedies.'*

Life is thrown into disarray once again when my lesbian friend disappears. We shared unique moments of intimacy, awakening each other and finding solace in each other's presence. She was a divorcee, and we both carried the weight of our own incompleteness. She too had her left breast removed. Through our shared experiences, we began to embrace our suppressed desires and rediscover the joy of physical connection. Much to my dismay, she has vanished unexpectedly from my life. The repeated disappearances and constant denial of love are infuriating me to a dangerous degree.

He steps into the void left by her disappearance, and after many years, I can sense his presence. He believed I had betrayed him during our college romance. However, his excitement reignites his love for me when he learns that I was forced into marriage under house arrest. When I saw him after a long time, the pain in my left breast was relieved. In fact, I don't have to feel any pain there because I don't even have a left breast. I felt relieved that the uneasiness that had gripped me, similar to phantom limb pain, had disappeared.

One day, she abruptly disappeared without informing me, even though we were in a warm relationship. I refused to lose hope. Every week, I visited the rented house where she was staying. The sight of a locked gate would dishearten me. This routine disappointment became a part of my life. After about two months, when new tenants arrived, I gave up even that occasional visit. Life has again become nothing but a senseless emptiness.

Now, I Am a Post-Surgery Bra...

- Height from ground about 25 feet

Buddha shares a wisdom in my diary that, *'Three things cannot be long hidden: the sun, the moon and the truth.'*

I was informed that my husband, the customs officer, will be transferred from Delhi and is returning home. After almost six years of living apart, we are finally going to resume living together. Typically, this news would bring joy to any wife. However, for me, it feels like a loss of freedom. Ever since I lost my left breast, he has been unable to satisfy me in bed. Now, all that remains is the responsibility of being a so-called good wife. This includes cooking and serving his favourite food, pressing his clothes without wrinkles, passing the television remote and finding his purse, belt, phone and specs. I am certain that my relationship with her will undergo significant changes once he returns. We will no longer be able to freely meet at my house or hers as we did before. Therefore, I perceive my husband's presence as a significant obstacle between us.

Do you know something? When I finally opened my eyes after a long period of sedation in the intensive care unit following my mastectomy, I found her lying on the bed next to me. She had also undergone a similar surgery. A satisfied expression adorned her face as she gazed at the white surface of the thermocol layers on the roof of the intensive care unit. I stared at her with the curiosity of a child seeing their mother for the first time. Occasionally, she would blink her eyes, though she remained under the effects of sedation and had not fully regained consciousness. Despite that, she appeared relaxed and serene. She was stretched out on the bed in a loose green gown that she had worn during the surgery, resembling a meadow gracefully swaying in the breeze.

No, I Am a Green Hospital Gown

- Height from ground about 20 feet.

Lewis Carroll chants in my diary, *'It's no use going back to yesterday, because I was a different person then.'*

It was during our hospital visits that we met and became friends. I vividly remember speaking to her for the first time during a break from pre-surgical counselling. She began to talk about her reluctance to remove the malignant breast.

'Let me get straight to the point. This isn't the first time cancer has spread in my body.'

'What?'

'Yes, I had to undergo a uterus removal due to cancer symptoms, which ultimately led to my divorce.'

'Sorry, I wasn't aware of that.'

'It's all right. But I am hesitant about having my left breast amputated at this time.'

'Why is that?'

'Even I don't know exactly. Let me share something else with you. I recall watching a French movie at a film festival, but I can't remember its title. There's a particular scene where the heroine experiences an orgasm. She walks through a bustling market, captivating the envious stares of onlookers fixated on her breasts. She then plunges her hands into the sacks of grains being sold, relishing the tactile sensation. I can resonate with that experience. I find a deep sense of pleasure when someone, regardless of their gender, appreciates my breasts through their gaze. It transports me to a majestic mountaintop, where I delicately balance on sharp rocks with one toe and extend my arms, gazing at the clouds above.'

'So, what?'

'Are you suggesting that I should relinquish all of this and return to a life without my left breast?'

'Please, we can't afford to wait. Treating the cancer is crucial for both of our survival.'

'Who lives longer for whom? Let me ask you one thing... If I have my left breast removed, can they guarantee that my right breast or other organs won't be affected by cancer?'

'Arguments or debates don't concern me. I came to see you on the doctor's advice. I can't even find a cause for the unexplained pain in my left breast. But I have made up my mind to do one thing: I am going to have it removed.'

'For the primary purpose of sustaining life, me too...'

'Me too...'

'Yes... Both of us... Together.'

Height from ground about 18 feet.

- I'm in the doctor's consulting room right now.

Kahlil Gibran offers solace in my diary, *'Your pain is the breaking of the shell that encloses your understanding. It is the bitter potion by which the physician within you heals your sick self. Therefore, trust the physician and drink his remedy in silence and tranquillity.'*

But I don't obey my physician.

'It's an unusual case. Not only I, but any doctor can't find any reason for it to be that dangerous. There's no need to worry so much. I have heard that in the United States, there have been cases where people opt for a mastectomy at the earliest signs of mild malignant symptoms. However, in our country, we haven't reached that stage yet. We will try all the best available options before considering a mastectomy. The pain you're experiencing in your left breast could also be psychological. Have you considered revisiting a consultation with a psychiatrist?'

'No, Doctor. I've reached my limit. After countless counselling sessions and treatments... I feel like I've become a helpless victim in this situation. I truly need a permanent solution.

'I can't bear the pain. Please remove my left breast.'

'Do you know the condition of the patient who left this room before me? She has cancer in her left breast and is in her mid-thirties, a divorcee with no children. Two years ago, she had to remove her uterus due to cancer. But even though she has been diagnosed with cancer in her left breast, she is against undergoing the surgery. In your case, things are different. Why don't you two talk to each other? She is also attending counselling sessions now. Having a conversation might be beneficial for both of you.'

Now, I Am a Kanchipuram Silk Marriage Sari...

- Height from ground about 15 feet

Leo Tolstoy reveals an absolute truth in my diary, '*All happy families are alike; each unhappy family is unhappy in its own way.*'

I am quarrelling with my husband.

'The doctor has already looked at the scan report and said that it's an issue that can be treated and cured. If there is anything more to it, they are merely your unnecessary emotions about it. It may be just a reflection of the lies you hold in your mind. That's what needs to be eliminated first.'

'Why are you not trying to understand my situation?'

'Okay, if you have to chop it off and become an Ottamulachi, just do it. You're a masochist...'

'I'm not a masochist who enjoys sex by wearing rings on the breast or naval, like the ones you see on the alternative lifestyle websites you're looking at. Yes, this may be a painful memory, but I am certain that it's not a lie. I feel the pain, otherwise, why would I request to simply remove an organ that is also a part of my womanhood?'

- I am trying to make love to my husband.

In the middle of foreplay, I find myself unable to continue due to the pain I'm experiencing. He touches my left breast, ignoring my repeated requests to stop. Ouch! It feels like a sharp needle is piercing through me. He claims that he needs to maintain his balance while being on top of me. Ah! Is this some sort of tightrope act?

'It's really sad that I can't even touch you without worrying. How can I know where to touch and where not to in this situation?'

'I'm sorry...'

'What's the use of saying sorry... I've lost my mood... Let me light a cigarette.'

'Oh, please...'

'Cut the crap and sleep now... Enough is enough.'

You may be wondering how he can treat a woman this way when he previously claimed to have complete authority over her, including financial activities. This is why a wise arbiter always emphasizes the importance of hearing both parties before reaching a conclusion. Also, it's important to consider that people can behave differently in various situations. They may become aggressive during intimate moments. These situations can sometimes reveal their true emotions and inner selves.

Now, I Am a Kalamkari Sari...

- Height from ground about 10 feet

Fyodor Dostoevsky's advice in my diary: *'There is also pleasure in a toothache. Here, of course, one does not remain silently angry, one moans; but these are not straightforward moans, they are crafty moans, and the craftiness is the whole point.'*

- I'm looking in the mirror at my aching left breast.

During my teenage years, as my breasts began to develop, there was no discomfort. Even as they reached full maturity, I experienced no pain. However, now, when I see my naked body or when someone touches my left breast, it triggers haunting memories of him. It feels like a dark shadow of a melancholic poem embedded on my left breast. It's as if the needle's tip touches the remnants of repressed anger. He betrayed my left breast with a kiss. I writhe in pain, feeling like I'm being crucified.

- I'm getting married.

Today is my wedding. The groom is a customs officer. I need to start a new life.

- I'm under house arrest.

When my parents discovered my love affair, they quickly took me away from the village. They imposed strict restrictions, forbidding me from leaving the house and confining me to a single room in our new home. The constant questioning, unsolicited advice and menacing threats have pushed me to the brink of madness. I had promised him we would reunite, but circumstances prevented me from keeping my word. Meanwhile, my parents have begun searching for marriage proposals without my consent. Among the choices they presented, I reluctantly chose the eldest and least attractive suitor. I am willing to exact revenge, even at the cost of my own happiness.

Now, I'm a Churidar with Embroidery...

- Height from ground about 7 feet

Bernard Shaw quips in my diary, *'First love is only a little foolishness and a lot of curiosity.'*

- I'm falling in love with him.

I first noticed him during an embarrassing moment. I had unintentionally said something with a double meaning, causing everyone to laugh. In that moment, he looked at me with remorse and silently tried to comfort me while others continued laughing. Later, I found a poem he had written in my notebook. It captivated my heart and made me fall deeply in love with him. From then on, he continued to write poems dedicated solely to me, expressing his love and admiration. Four years of love passed, and numerous poems were born during that time.

- I'm parting with him.

On my final day in college, I sat alone in a quiet corner of the library. He shared with me the last poem he had written, which was about Lilith. Until then, I had no knowledge of who Lilith was. His poetry depicted Lilith in a way that challenged society's common perception of her as evil. In his verses, all women were portrayed as different facets of me, including Lilith. Religious texts like the Bible and Talmud describe Lilith as engaging in predatory behaviour. This includes mating with sleeping men and harming children. She is portrayed as a rapacious daemon with long, dark hair. However, in his poetry, she was exquisitely beautiful, just like me. She represented Adam's first wife, a woman who chose to live independently without submitting to Adam or his God. Lilith was expelled from Eden for boldly addressing God by name without reverence.

I was completely immersed in that poem when suddenly, he tried to hug and kiss me. I reflexively stepped back, not expecting it, and his kiss landed on my left breast. I became nervous and quickly leaned against a shelf stacked with books, causing a row of books to topple. I hastily left the library before the librarian arrived, alerted by the sound of falling books. As I walked away, I turned around and smiled at the sight of him picking up his books in total panic.

Now, I'm a Pleated Pink Skirt...

- Height from ground about 5 feet.

Edgar Allan Poe agrees with me in my diary, '*The best things in life make you sweaty.*'

- I'm getting my first period.

I am an 8th grade student sitting in my classroom, focusing on my history textbook. The teacher is discussing Akkamma Cheriyan, a freedom fighter known as the Jhansi Rani of Travancore. As the teacher speaks, I picture Akkamma in my mind, riding a horse and charging towards the king of Travancore's police force. Suddenly, I find myself on the horse instead of Akkamma. I tremble atop the fast-moving horse, feeling pain in my chest and abdomen. Snapping out of this vision, I quickly stand up in the classroom. My chest is swelling, my stomach is cramping, and my uniform is wet with sweat. Feeling upset, I ask the teacher for permission to go to the toilet. There, I realize I'm experiencing signs of my own growth.

Now, I Am a Colourful Frock

- Height from ground about 1 foot.

Charles Darwin proclaims in my diary, *'I long to set foot where no man has trod before.'*

- I'm starting to walk for the first time.

While crawling on all fours, I lose my balance and fall. Gradually, I manage to stand up. I start walking slowly on soft feet across the rain-soaked earth in the courtyard.

Now I'm Completely Naked

- I'm at ground level right now.

Here I am, born into a world teeming with billions of lives, both visible and invisible, small and large.

Finally, I jot down in my diary, 'I realize that my story, presented in fragmented pages of the book of life, remains incomplete. I urge you to read it alongside other lessons as stories find their completeness through multiple interpretations.'

At ground level, I kiss the soil, feeling connected by the umbilical cord. I'm born upside down on this Earth and start crying. The slimy blood that coats a newborn baby also covers me now.

Now, you may think that you have reached the end of the story and finished this book. But you must understand that you have just delved into the opening chapter of my life's book... Ta-da!

Exercise

I. Can you provide a brief overview of Lilith, incorporating some information about her mythological origins, folkloric portrayals and contemporary political implications?

Ans:

In mythology, Lilith, Adam's first wife, was created from the same clay as him. She demanded equality in their relationship and rejected subservience to him. Lilith's rebellion against Adam's dominance is often seen as an early expression of feminist ideals. It challenges traditional gender roles and asserts her autonomy. In some versions of the myth, Lilith chose to leave the Garden of Eden rather than bow to Adam's authority. She sought freedom and independence beyond the confines of a patriarchal society. Lilith is frequently associated with darkness and night, symbolizing the primal and untamed aspects of femininity often suppressed by society.

Lilith is often depicted as a seductive and enchanting figure. Her captivating beauty conceals a dangerous and malevolent nature. In later folklore, Lilith is linked to newborn misfortunes and seen as a temptress who leads men to ruin. Her association with evil stems from her defiance against societal norms and refusal to conform to male expectations. Lilith is sometimes represented as a demonic figure with wings and a serpent-like appearance, symbolizing her rebellious nature. Despite her negative portrayal, some feminist interpretations reclaim Lilith as a symbol of female empowerment. They celebrate her refusal to compromise her individuality and her challenge to oppressive societal structures. In contemporary times, Lilith has become an iconic figure. She inspires artists, writers and feminists to explore themes of female agency, sexuality and resistance against patriarchal norms.

II. Write a brief note about the mythical figure Ottamulachi.

Ans:

The mythical figure Ottamulachi is a fearsome character in various myths and legends. Often depicted as a daemon, Ottamulachi has dishevelled hair, glowing eyes and a single breast in the centre of her chest. She is accompanied by wild animals and is known for seducing men, killing them and drinking their blood. However, a legend suggests Ottamulachi is the incarnation of Kannaki, the heroic figure from the Tamil epic Chilapathikaram. According to this legend, Kannaki sought revenge against the Pandya king who mistakenly killed her husband, believing him a thief. In her fury, she plucked and discarded her own breast, using its power to destroy the kingdom.

Interestingly, Ottamulachi is also worshipped in certain regions, highlighting the complex nature of this mythical figure.

III. In this chapter, you must have learned about the woman who experiences pain in her left breasts even after a mastectomy, haven't you? Write a short description of what a phantom limb is and explain the Mirror-Box Experiment conducted by Vilayanur S. Ramachandran. Please collect and paste any relevant images, if necessary.

Phantom limb phenomenon, or phantom pain, refers to a sensation experienced by amputees. They feel as if their amputated limb is still present, despite its physical absence. This can occur after the removal of any body part.

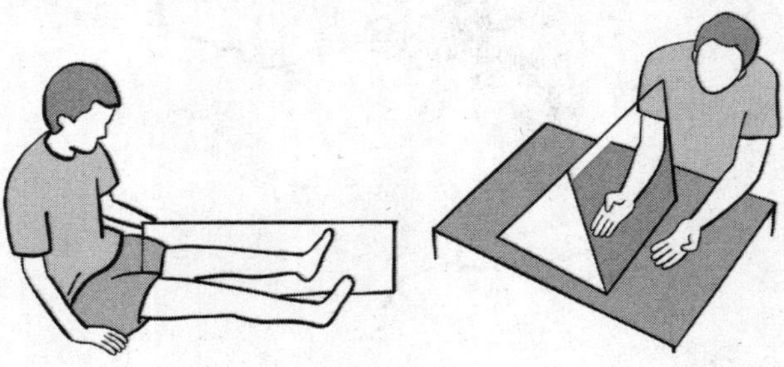

The exact cause of phantom pain is not fully understood, but it is believed to involve a rewiring of nerves in the spinal cord and brain in response to the loss of signals from the missing limb.

Famous neuroscientist Vilayanur S. Ramachandran conducted a research experiment called the Mirror-Box Experiment. In this experiment, a mirror box serves as a tool to alleviate phantom limb pain. The patient places their intact limb inside the box. The amputated limb is positioned in front of the mirror, creating a visual illusion of the missing limb.

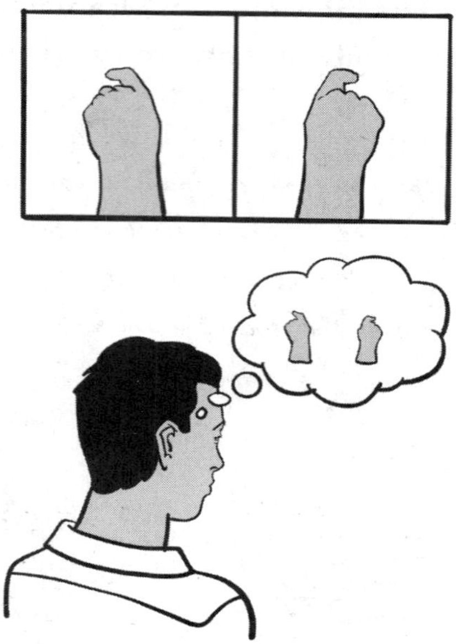

During the experiment, the patient moves their intact limb while observing its reflection in the mirror. This creates the illusion that the amputated limb is also moving. As a result, the brain perceives this visual feedback and begins to integrate the visual and motor signals. This integration often leads to a reduction in phantom limb pain.

IV. What are the distinguishing factors between accidental death and suicide when a person appears to have fallen from the top of a building and died?

Ans:

Position: *The body's position, especially the face, can provide clues about whether the person fell accidentally or jumped intentionally.*

Autopsy and forensics: *These are crucial in determining the cause of death. They reveal fall or self-inflicted injuries. The type and severity of injuries can indicate an accidental fall or an intentional jump. The presence of drugs or alcohol in the body is also crucial in decision-making.*

Mental state: *Investigators search for personal items or past events, like medications, prescriptions and medical records, that might indicate an unstable mental state.*

Witnesses: *Statements from witnesses can provide valuable information.*

Circumstances: *Investigators verify the reasons leading up to the event. They search for any sign of premeditation, such as a suicide note.*

IV. Draw a character relationship diagram based on the places and characters from different chapters. Mark the direct and indirect relationships separately.

Ans: *(see diagram on the facing page)*

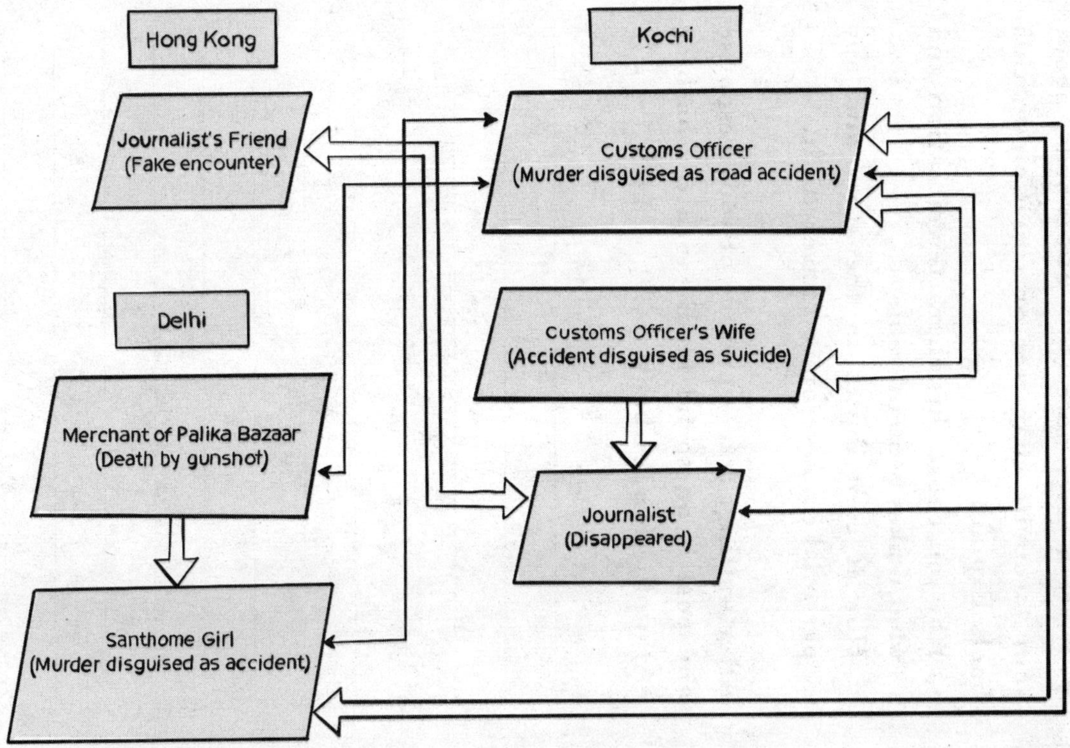
Hong Kong
Kochi
Journalist's Friend
(Fake encounter)
Customs Officer
(Murder disguised as road accident)
Delhi
Customs Officer's Wife
(Accident disguised as suicide)
Merchant of Palika Bazaar
(Death by gunshot)
Journalist
(Disappeared)
Santhome Girl
(Murder disguised as accident)

V. Write a brief note (150–200 words) about your favourite character or situation in this book. Explain:

- **Why you chose this character/situation and what makes it memorable.**
- **How it contributes to the story and any personal connection you have with it.**

After writing, take a picture of your response and post it on social media with the hashtag #APulpFictionTextbook.

The Curious Incident of the Dog in the Night-Time
GCSE Student Edition

Simon Stephens began his theatrical career in the literary department of the Royal Court Theatre, where he ran its Young Writers' Programme. His plays for theatre include *Bluebird; Herons; Port; One Minute; Christmas; Country Music; On the Shore of the Wide World; Motortown; Pornography; Harper Regan; Sea Wall; Heaven; Punk Rock; The Trial of Ubu; A Thousand Stars Explode in the Sky* (co-written with David Eldridge and Robert Holman); *Marine Parade* (co-written with Mark Eitzel); *T5; Wastwater; Morning*; an adaptation of *A Doll's House; Blindsided*; and *Birdland*. Awards include the Pearson Award for Best New Play, 2001, for *Port;* Olivier Award for Best New Play for *On the Shore of the Wide World*, 2005; and German critics in Theater Heute's annual poll voted him Best Foreign Playwright, 2007, for *Motortown*. His adaptation of *The Curious Incident of the Dog in the Night-Time* won the 2015 Tony Award for Best Play.

Jacqueline Bolton is Lecturer in Drama and Theatre at the University of Lincoln. Her research interests include contemporary British theatre, dramaturgy and new writing. She has published in the journal *Contemporary Theatre Review*, is the editor of the Methuen Drama Student Edition of *Pornography* by Simon Stephens, and author of 'Joint Stock' in *British Theatre Companies: 1980–1994*, edited by Graham Saunders (Bloomsbury Methuen Drama, 2015). She is associate editor of the journal *Studies in Theatre and Performance*.

Mark Haddon is the author of *The Red House, A Spot of Bother* and *The Curious Incident of the Dog in the Night-Time*. He has also published a collection of poetry, *The Talking Horse and the Sad Girl and the Village Under the Sea*. His work for television and radio includes *Coming Down the Mountain and Microsoap*. *Polar Bears* (2010) was Mark Haddon's first work for the theatre.

Methuen Drama publications for GCSE students

Available and forthcoming

GCSE Student Editions

Willy Russell's *Blood Brothers*

Simon Stephens's *The Curious Incident of the Dog in the Night-Time*, adapted from the novel by Mark Haddon

Charlotte Keatley's *My Mother Said I Never Should*

Shelagh Delaney's *A Taste of Honey*

GCSE Student Guides

Willy Russell's *Blood Brothers* by Ros Merkin

Simon Stephens's *The Curious Incident of the Dog in the Night-Time* by Jacqueline Bolton, adapted from the novel by Mark Haddon

Dennis Kelly's *DNA* by Maggie Inchley

Alan Bennett's *The History Boys* by Steve Nicholson

J. B. Priestley's *An Inspector Calls* by Philip Roberts

R. C. Sherriff's *Journey's End* by Andrew Maunder

Charlotte Keatley's *My Mother Said I Never Should* by Sophie Bush

Shelagh Delaney's *A Taste of Honey* by Kate Whittaker